Whistle in the Dark

By the same author

The House In Abercromby Square
The Manchester Affair
Shadow of Dark Water
Mistress of Luke's Folly
The Rose Hedge

Elizabeth Elgin

WHISTLE IN THE DARK

ROBERT HALE · LONDON

ISBN 0 7091 5563 8

Robert Hale Limited
Clerkenwell House
Clerkenwell Green
London EC1R 0HT

Printed in Great Britain by
St Edmundsbury Press Limited, Bury St Edmunds, Suffolk.
Bound by WBC Book Manufacturers Limited
Bridgend, Mid Glamorgan.

ONE

Edwina's phone call was all I could remember clearly about yesterday. In my confused, frightened mind it stood out safe and sane like candleglow in the darkness. I had clutched it to me as a frightened child grasps comforting hands when it awakens from a nightmare, and yesterday — all of yesterday — had been a nightmare.

I leaned back and closed my eyes, surrendering to the noisy rocking of the train as it hurtled northwards, letting the hiss of wheels on steel vibrate in my head and block out all chance of coherent thought.

"An abandoned Land-Rover means nothing at all, Mrs Parr," the man from Johnny's firm had said gently. "We shall soon hear that he is safe and well, be sure of it."

But then he told me they had found Johnny's coat a little way off with his wallet in the inside pocket, untouched. Whatever had happened in that isolated part of Iran, robbery had not been the motive.

Iran. The word danced vaguely in and out of my mind. Why had Johnny been in Iran when he disappeared? The oil company he worked for had sent him to Abu Dhabi, hadn't they?

"There will be some quite simple explanation," the kindly, grey-haired man had insisted. "You know, you shouldn't be alone," he urged gently. "Can I get in touch with your parents or a relative, perhaps?"

But I'd had to tell him that apart from Johnny there was no one. There might have been our son; the little stillborn baby who had caused our marriage.

5

I opened my eyes, then blinked rapidly against threatening tears, biting on my lip until it hurt. I wouldn't cry. Self-pity was something I could do well without. Facts were there to be faced and fact was that my husband had disappeared.

But it wasn't as simple as that, or why did I feel a strange crawling under my skin? What primitive instinct warned that something was wrong? Why couldn't my reason let me accept the situation for what it was?

I sat in the empty flat unmoving, long after the man had gone, staring numbly into the empty coffee-mug. Had he, in his kindness, mistaken my lack of emotion for grief? I remembered him spooning sugar generously into the drink he made me, thinking perhaps that that was the right thing to do in cases of shock. But I hadn't been in shock—just paralysed, almost, by a feeling of imminent danger. I was afraid and my fear was not for Johnny but for myself. Johnny's eyes had watched me from every corner of that darkening room and Johnny's voice whispered mockingly from the past, *"They'll never get me, Kathleen. The devil takes care of his own"*. Johnny wouldn't let himself get hurt or lost. He could take care of himself without any help at all from the devil.

I felt ashamed and vaguely surprised that I had not been able to find pity for my husband. It made me feel slightly unreal. But would any real woman have sat there befuddled, cringing from the shadows? A real woman would have . . . What *would* she have done? I honestly didn't know.

I had jumped to my feet then, snapping on all the lights in the room, closing the curtains on the grey November afternoon, shutting out the eyes that seemed to watch and mock me and all the while grieving because I could feel no grief.

What could I do? Apart from Johnny I was quite alone

and there was no one I could turn to. A small pulse of panic beat in my throat and I fought down the feeling to run; away from the flat; away from a fear that was so real I could almost smell it. But I couldn't leave—not yet. There was something I must do before I packed my cases and turned my back on reality.

It lay on the mantelshelf beside the flowered paper-weight—left where I would be sure to find it—the key to Johnny's desk. I hadn't picked it up because I knew that that was what he had wanted me to do. He had wanted me to open his desk, and when I did I knew now that I would find something there that was evil and menacing. It wasn't my overworked imagination that made me feel the way I did. Johnny's desk had always been a private thing and he'd never once left the key behind him. I'd been a little apprehensive when he did but I hadn't worried too much about it—not until the man from the welfare department of Eastern Oil Inc. called at the flat to tell me that my husband was missing in questionable circumstances in a strange country. That was when the awful fear really exploded inside me.

So after the well-meaning little man left me staring into the bright red coffee-mug, I knew I had to look inside the desk. Johnny had deliberately left the key. Johnny never did anything without a reason and to find that reason I had only to slip the small, intricately fashioned key into the lock. . . .

Do it, Kathy, my mind urged. *It's only an ordinary key that opens an ordinary desk.*

Stupidly I crossed my fingers as I had done in childhood, then, half-mesmerised, I stretched out my hand and picked up the key.

It didn't burn my fingers as I imagined it would; it didn't feel particularly cold, either. It was only a key, I told myself yet again. What harm could there be in it? But for all that, the spittle of fear filled my mouth. I swallowed hard and noisily, then, taking a deep breath, walked slowly across the room.

As I turned the key and slowly lowered the flap, I wanted to laugh with hysterical relief, for there was no ghoul crouched inside, waiting to spring at my throat; no tightly coiled snake ready to lift its head with the speed of a lightning flash and dart a venomous tongue at me; no stench of evil. Writing-paper and envelopes were neatly placed in pigeon-holes and on the inkstand lay two newly sharpened pencils and Johnny's gold-plated pen. Everything seemed very ordinary and normal; even the blotting-paper had been renewed and lay there, white and clean, awaiting its owner's return.

I saw it then — the long, slim envelope, hardly noticeable against the blotter, with my name, written bold and black in Johnny's handwriting, seeming suddenly to spring shrieking into focus.

Kathleen.

I looked at my name for a long time, calming myself, willing my heartbeats to become less frantic.

So this, I thought dully, is the reason for it all. This is why Johnny allowed me to trespass into his jealously guarded privacy; a white envelope with my name sprawled across it. Now perhaps I would know why he was missing, why he had travelled to Iran and not to Abu Dhabi; what was in his complex mind. I might even find inside it the reason for the cold fear that tingled from my head to my toes and refused to be ignored.

Clumsily my fingers ripped at the envelope. The letter I had expected to find was not there; only a folded piece of paper that bore a number and a name and address — my name and address. It was a little while before I realised I had been looking at the statement of a deposit account.

At first, I was sure that someone had made a mistake,

8

for the amount it contained was, according to the figures printed neatly and impersonally, so utterly unbelievable that I wanted to laugh out loud.

Then cold, calm logic took over. Suddenly I knew it was all real, all part of the reason for my fear and apprehension. People like Johnny didn't have that kind of money. People like him who asserted that money was for spending just didn't have the prudence to save so great a sum and, if he had, he wouldn't have placed it secretly in the name of a wife he despised almost to the point of loathing.

The diesel-express crashed and swayed across a set of points, jerking my mind back to the present, causing me to turn my head to where fields and trees and telegraph poles slipped past the window of the compartment in a normal, ordinary manner.

Did they, I wondered, those women who glanced up idly from their washing-lines as the long, twisting train snaked past them, ever wonder about the people inside it and where they were going, and why? But they were uncomplicated women, most likely, whose husbands would be home that night and who hadn't found fourteen thousand pounds in a bank account they hadn't known to exist.

"Tomorrow?" the bank manager suggested when I had phoned him early next morning. "At three o'clock . . .?"

"No, I'm sorry, but it can't wait that long. It'll have to be today—this morning, if possible. It's urgent, you see. I must go away . . ."

There had been the barest of pauses, then:

"Very well, Mrs Parr. Immediately after lunch, at two?"

I had hoped for an earlier appointment but I hadn't the inclination to argue and anyway, I reasoned, I could spend the ~ainder of the morning packing and getting ready to go. ~ was I going? I didn't know and I didn't care. ~ been to the bank I would take the first

9

train out of Euston and that would be that. I had to get out of the flat—out of London—find some quiet place where I could think straight and where the smell of danger unseen was not so sickeningly strong. I had a little money of my own that would see me through for a few weeks; I'd manage, somehow.

And not once during that morning of frantic packing had I stopped to think a little, to stand aside from the situation in which I found myself and try to take stock of events. Perhaps if I had done that, if I had taken a deep breath and counted up to ten and tried to look facts in the face, I might well have been able to reassure myself a little, calm the terrible panic that seemed to be in absolute possession of my every action and my very reason.

But I couldn't do that because I could only feel now the trapped bewilderment of a hunted animal. Johnny should have been foremost in my thoughts. I should have worried for his safety and willed him home again. But all my fears were for myself because I knew I must escape the danger that every instinct told me was all around me.

Nor did the bank manager, when I met him, do anything at all to help allay my fears. He settled me in a chair, then offered me a cigarette before sitting down at his desk.

"Can you explain this to me?" I demanded at once, handing the statement to him.

I knew immediately from the guarded look on his face that he felt uncomfortable about it. He said:

"Ah, yes. Mr John Parr and the Lowry."

"The Lowry?" I repeated, annoyed with myself because I sounded so stupid.

"Yes," he nodded, "Your husband sold it. You knew, of course?"

For a few stupefied seconds my mind refused to function, then I recalled the Northern artist and his paintings of mill-chimneys and crowded market places and alleys, all busy with little stiff figures.

"Of course," I said slowly, "the Lowry."

There was a look of apprehension in the manager's eyes, almost as if he could guess I was playing for time. He looked at me as if the truth was written in inch-high letters across my forehead.

I don't understand. I don't know what you are talking about!

But it wasn't emblazoned there so I said:

"To be quite honest, I'm still a bit surprised."

Something inside warned me to tread gently.

"You didn't think it would bring so much, eh, Mrs Parr?"

I was being quizzed, I knew it. Like me, this man had doubts about something, so I didn't reply; I merely smiled and shrugged my shoulders.

"I don't suppose Mr Parr's parents realised its value, either," he pressed. "You know, it makes one wonder how many more families in the North have an early Lowry tucked away somewhere, completely unaware of its value."

I nodded and gave him a little smile.

"I certainly didn't realise we had a painting like that," I probed.

For a moment neither of us spoke and I was almost certain that the man who sat opposite me had some vague idea that perhaps my apparent stupidity was caused by sheer surprise at my good fortune.

I shrugged inside me. If that were so, I might be able to learn the truth of the matter without admitting my absolute ignorance of it.

"Who bought the painting?" I asked, as briskly as I could.

"Now there, Mrs Parr, I'm afraid I can't help you. Your husband did, in fact, present me with fourteen thousand

11

pounds in notes and I'll admit that at the time I wasn't entirely satisfied with his explanation."

Obviously uncomfortable, he tried to smile.

"You see, when a transaction such as that takes place, it is unusual for a buyer—who in this case I was given to understand was an American gentleman—to produce such a large amount in sterling."

He cleared his throat and looked down, embarrassed, at his fingers.

"And there's the matter of tax liability on such a sale. To be quite frank with you, Mrs Parr, I got the impression that the whole transaction was—well—under the counter, so to speak. I took it upon myself to explain the tax position to your husband at the time."

"Yes, I'm sure you did everything possible. I think my husband is well aware of his liabilities," I hazarded, guiltily warming to my own deceit. "Let's hope so," I added, trying hard to sound unconcerned.

"Yes indeed."

The bank manager was relieved, no doubt, that he had had his say and, to some extent, cleared his professional conscience.

"And you will treat this meeting as confidential, Mrs Parr? I have the idea, you see, that your husband didn't want you—well, that he wanted all this to be a surprise for you . . ."

He nodded his head like an ancient sage then looked me squarely between the eyes for the first time since our interview began.

". . . I mean, placing the money in *your* name—"

Oh, he didn't have to hedge so delicately. I knew exactly what he was implying; trying to tell me in such carefully chosen words that something was very wrong about the whole thing. Whether he had already decided that I was a willing party to it, I didn't know.

I rose to my feet, glad again that he couldn't see inside my head, and held out my hand.

"Thank you," I replied, hardly daring to meet his eyes. "I'm grateful to you and I shall certainly respect your confidence. I'll probably put the statement back where I found it, and that will be the end of the matter."

But I couldn't do that, I knew it. I had destroyed the envelope and it didn't matter one way or the other since Johnny intended all along that I should find it.

Bemused, I waved my hand at a cruising taxi and was thankful when the driver pulled in at the kerb, for my legs felt weak and I was now almost incapable of thinking straight.

So Johnny had secretly sold an original painting left to him by his North-country parents and put the proceeds in his wife's name with an excess of marital affection? All very plausible, of course, had his parents come from the North. But they hadn't. Johnny's people were Londoners born and bred, who had both been killed in the blitz, and everything they owned, Johnny said, had been bombed into rubble. Whoever had handed fourteen thousand pounds in old notes to Johnny had not done so in exchange for a painting, for the simple reason that I knew without the shadow of a doubt that my husband had never owned so much as a Lowry reproduction, far less an early original.

Where the money had come from or from whom, I had no way of knowing. One thing only filled my mind as the taxi pulled out of the slow-moving traffic and turned into the side road that led to our flat: *I had to get away*. I didn't know what I was running from or where I could run to, but a primitive fear that defied all reason thrashed uncontrollably inside me and I knew I had to obey it.

Taking a deep breath, I tried to think more calmly. From somewhere Johnny had got hold of a great deal of money; not money slowly and laboriously saved but fourteen thousand pounds from the sale of a non-existent painting. That money had been placed in an account in my name and I hadn't been told about it — at least, not until Johnny decided I should be.

Now Johnny was missing. A car he had hired and his coat — containing ample identification — had been found in Iran when the destination on his air ticket had been Abu Dhabi. Add to that the fact that for a long time Johnny and I had been polite strangers, living out each of his leaves with a tension between us that almost screamed its presence, and I was left once more with the age-old instinct that warned me I should have to keep my head if I wanted to survive.

Those feelings that churned inside me had not been born of sorrow at the loss of my child or of a hurt bewilderment at the withdrawing of Johnny's love for me. They had not come about because an ardent lover had suddenly, without apparent reason, become an intolerant husband. Those feelings were animal and primitive and inexplicable and I knew I must obey them without question.

Hastily I jumped from the cab, thrusting a note at the driver, indicationg that he should keep the change.

My trembling fingers guided the latch-key into the lock and I glanced again around the familiar flat. Nothing had changed yet everything was different. There was a truculence about the place, a strange brooding silence that warned me that I was no longer a part of it. My eyes alighted on the soft walnut glow of Johnny's desk and suddenly it became a hostile thing.

I opened my handbag and took out the bank statement. I had intended to put it back in the desk, but now I decided against it. I wanted, for a brief moment, to burn it into unrecognisable ashes. Then sanity prevailed and I hurriedly stuffed it back into my handbag. I was wasting time; my packing was still unfinished. I almost ran into the bedroom, looking around me fearfully, flinging wide the wardrobe doors, glancing into mirrors and over my shoulder, all the while not knowing what I expected to find or to see. Soon I would lose control and give way to sobbing hysteria. Desperately I stuffed a fist into my mouth and bit on my knuckles. Then the telephone had started to ring.

"Edwina? Oh, Edwina! Why did you call? I mean, it's been ages," I faltered, grateful beyond belief for her detached sanity.

"Almost three years, lovey," she had replied. "Just before you were married, wasn't it?"

"But how did you *know*? Did you get some telepathic message, or something?"

I could have sobbed with relief.

"Something like that. I just had a sudden urge to talk to you, Kathy. You sound funny. *Is* anything wrong?"

"*Wrong?* Oh, Edwina, you've no idea *how* wrong! Johnny's missing!"

"Missing?"

I heard the faint hiss of her indrawn breath.

"Yes. A man from the oil company came yesterday to tell me. They've found the car he was driving and his coat, somewhere in Iran. I don't understand it. I don't know what to believe," I finished, confused.

"Listen, Kathy." The flippancy had gone now from Edwina's voice. "Take a deep breath and begin at the beginning . . ."

So I had stumblingly told her what the welfare man from Eastern Oil had told me and she listened without interrupting.

"You'd better come to me," she said without preamble when I had finished. "Come up to Slaidbeck. Get an early train tomorrow morning. There's one about nine, I think, from King's Cross."

15

Gratefully I had done as she said. Quickly I finished my packing, then phoned a hotel near the station and booked in for the night. I had been determined to leave the flat at once and nothing had happened — not even Edwina's phone call — to make me change my mind. I couldn't stay in it another night. Automatically I checked that everything was turned off and that all the windows were secure, then, scribbling a note for the milkman, I sighed with inward relief. One more thing remained to be done. Slowly and quite deliberately I placed the little key in the desk lock and left it there. When — if — Johnny returned to the flat he would know I had received his cryptic message. It would be up to him, then, to find me. And even if he did, it wouldn't matter because by then I would be safe, with Edwina.

Dear Edwina. In less than an hour my train would be in Leeds and perhaps she would be waiting for me there. Edwina Howarth — bossy, self-sufficient, pride of the hockey team, head girl of the school. Edwina, my dearest friend, behind whose personality I had always sheltered. Why, then, hadn't I told her about the key and the money and about Johnny's strange moods? Why did I only tell her what the oil company had told me and about the baby I had lost? Had I imagined in my apprehension that perhaps even the walls were listening to our conversation? Had I really been so terrified that I had been afraid to tell even Edwina? But when we were together, when I had lost myself in the wilds of North Yorkshire, when I was safe again, I would be able to tell her everything. She had a right to know, after all, just what she was taking on. But oh, it would be good to see her again and to remember our schooldays together. Orphans of the Storm, she had called us. I hadn't really been an orphan then, as she was. My parents were in India. They had scraped my boarding-school fees from their meagre earnings at the mission

16

hospital, telling themselves no doubt that they were doing what was best for me. I was born to them in their middle years and I think it was a relief when the decision to leave me behind in England had been made and they could return to their beloved India. A vague remembrance of our goodbye in Matron's room was all I could recall of them, now.

I didn't see them again. They died later of cholera within a few days of each other, but at least I had known them. Edwina had not been so lucky. She had no one — not even a memory. Accounts for school fees and indeed for everything else she needed were paid for by the faceless solicitor who administered the trust fund set up by the parents she had never known.

Once, we talked together of what we wanted from life when we grew up. I had settled, quite promptly, for a husband and three babies. I think even then I'd yearned to belong, to have someone to protect and cosset me — someone who cared.

Edwina's reply had not been so forthcoming.

"I don't know yet what I want to do or to be," she said, eventually, "but whatever it is, I want to do it successfully. Yes, that's what I shall be, Kathy — a success!"

She had gone into the fashion business — the Rag Trade as she flippantly called it — and I married Johnny. But I hadn't found love or protection and our child had not lived.

It still hurt to remember the night I rushed sobbing from the flat with Johnny's taunts winging after me. I had stumbled and fallen and our little boy was stillborn, two days later. I had begged Johnny's forgiveness then, promising another child, but I think I had known our marriage was a sham, long before that nightmare happened.

I shrugged away the memory, looking with disinterest at

the empty fields and sleeping, leafless trees as they slipped past my fixed gaze.

Now I was running away from memories of Johnny. I had failed utterly whilst Edwina was the success she predicted so long ago in that darkened dormitory, with a chain of boutiques in the North that made news in the glossy magazines. Edwina Howarth's name carried weight in the world of fashion. I was glad she was my friend; grateful she had phoned me from out of nowhere when I needed not to be alone. She was strong and self-reliant and exactly the person I needed. Edwina had always known what to do; Edwina would understand.

I looked at my watch, impatient to be there. The hands pointed to five minutes after midday. Soon, I would have to change trains.

"I don't think I'll be able to make it to Leeds," Edwina said, "but I'll be waiting for you at Skipton. Can you manage all right?" she had urged, thinking no doubt that I was that same helpless Kathy of our schooldays. An unsure, insecure girl who had been glad to be Edwina Howarth's shadow. And I was still the same person, or why was I behaving so stupidly? Why was I running away? Johnny had secretly despised me, of that I was sure, and who could honestly blame him?

I rummaged in my handbag and took out my compact, holding it away from me until the whole of my face was caught in the tiny mirror. Idly I flicked away the hair that hung limp over my face; hair that once had danced with chestnut lights. I was twenty-three, yet the two years I had been married to Johnny seemed like two lifetimes. I felt I had never been young.

I went through the motions of dabbing at my nose and chin, then smeared on more lipstick. It was pale pink and quite the wrong colour for me, but it didn't seem to matter any more.

Now the November fields had given way to rows of tiny houses where limp washing hung in winter-drab gardens. It all seemed a million miles from the sun-scorched outcrop in Iran that had last seen Johnny.

I shut down my thoughts. I wouldn't think about it any more. I would wait and tell it to Edwina — all of it. Edwina would straighten things out.

I jumped to my feet, steadying myself against the lurching of the train as it slowed down at the approaches to the station, tugging my cases from the rack.

Great grey buildings loomed past and a haze of grime hung over chimneys that stood tall on either side of the track.

"Change trains at Leeds," Edwina had said. With new resolve, I picked up my cases.

As usual, porters seemed not to notice me, but I found a seat eventually on the little local train that would take me on the last part of my journey and soon the city was slipping behind us, the gaunt chimneys yielding to trim estates of well-kept houses. Then suburbia was suddenly gone and in the distance hills loomed dark and aloof. On either side of the track stretched miles of open country, dotted with isolated houses built solid of stone, their slate roofs shining wet in the pale sunlight that cut the misty air. Huddles of black-faced sheep cropped the thin winter grass and a flock of starlings rose startled and winged away from the whine of the train.

The sudden stark beauty gave me a strange uplift of hope. Soon, I was certain, the oil company would tell me that Johnny was on his way home and it had all been a mistake. Perhaps then I would be able to talk things out with him; try at least to wrest some understanding from the near-chaos our marriage had become. But would it work out? I could try to forgive but had I courage enough to forget? Could I put behind me all the small taunts, the silences that had been between us or Johnny's unspoken contempt? And would Johnny want to try again? He had the ability, it seemed, to withstand the silences between us better than I. Each time he returned on leave from some Middle East oilfield I had felt for a little time some faint hope that this once things would be better. But always Johnny became restless, leaving the flat for hours at a time, offering no explanation on his return, lapsing into silences I could not penetrate. And after the silences would come the whistling.

Johnny had always whistled when he was in a cruel mood —always the same tune. He'd done it first to hurt me. Once, I had found the fleeting courage to tell him I was leaving. Hot, bitter tears flowed down my face as I packed a case, throwing in my clothes blindly, haphazardly. And Johnny had watched me, indolently leaning on the bedroom door, whistling that tune . . .

I'll take you home again, Kathleen,
Across the ocean wild and wide . . .

Johnny had known how to hurt; known there was no home for me to run to, no parents to give me sympathy or comfort. He knew I was alone, that I was timid and afraid of life and would settle, in the end, for the devil I knew.

I'll take you home again, Kathleen . . . Johnny could besmirch even the sweetest of love-songs.

Tears knotted themselves into a tight ball in my throat and I closed my eyes tightly and swallowed hard. Soon I would be at Skipton and Edwina would be waiting for me. Soon, I could reach back to my schooldays where constantly ringing bells had regulated my life, where Matron was always at hand in her cosy room, where once I had been content to let Edwina's vibrant personality wrap me round and hide me. Soon now, I would be safe.

20

TWO

Edwina was waiting on the platform looking composed and elegant — exactly as I had expected she would. She smiled as our eyes met and lifted her hand in greeting, then, with the barest nod of her head, brought a porter hurrying to her side.

Eagerly I started towards her, arms outstretched.

"Oh, Edwina, it's been so long! It's so good to see you!"

I flung my arms around her neck and felt her cool, detached kiss on my cheek.

She held me at arm's length.

"Your lipstick's a mess," she said, and I laughed out loud with joy. She hadn't changed. She was still the safe, sane Edwina who could make a criticism sound like sisterly appraisal. Everything would start to come right now, I was absolutely sure of it and, as I had always done in the old days, I followed happily behind her.

Taking the ticket from my hand, she broke it crisply into two, giving one half to the collector at the barrier and handing the other back to me.

"Put it in your purse — safely," she said with mock severity and we burst into peals of laughter. I wanted to hug her again, just because I suddenly felt so safe. Her presence seemed to have blotted out the unhappiness and bewilderment of the past two years. It seemed that by just being there she could calm my fears and take me back to the softly cushioned world of our shooldays. I wanted to tell her so, but she was busy with the porter.

"In here, please."

Edwina unlocked the boot of the long, low car and saw my cases safely inside. Then she took off her sheepskin coat and tossed it carelessly on to the back seat.

Expertly she nosed the car into the traffic, then glanced sideways at me, briefly.

"All right?"

I nodded contentedly, happy not to talk.

Edwina was dressed superbly. Her clothes identified with the country life she was now living but they were not in the least bit dull. Her skirt of soft, fine tweed was beautifully cut and its matching sweater in palest cream cashmere hugged her slight figure.

Coral lipstick, the only make-up she wore, matched exactly the long ropes of beads hung round her neck, and knee-length boots of softest kid looked as if they had been moulded to her long, shapely legs.

She negotiated a roundabout and swung to the left.

"I like your hair," I ventured.

It was short and simple — so deceptively simple that it could only have been the product of very skilled and expensive cutting.

Her only acknowledgement was a slight raising of her eyebrows and she did not speak again until the old market town was well behind us and we were heading for open country.

"Sorry I couldn't meet you in Leeds, Kathy."

Edwina offered no explanation, but then, she never did.

"That's all right."

I didn't mind. I was on my way back to Slaidbeck and London and all its problems seemed a long way away. It was a relief to be able to relax a little.

With Edwina's capable hands on the wheel of the powerful car, the miles slipped smoothly past. Now the moors stretched all around us and I wondered what it would be like to be stranded in the middle of all this savage grandeur. Involuntarily, my eyes searched for the fuel-gauge. It pointed to almost-full. But then, I reasoned, I should have known that it would.

A signpost at the crossing of two narrow moorland roads indicated that Slaidbeck was ten miles away.

I glanced at Edwina. She had lapsed once more into near-silence, speaking only to point out briefly something of interest; a particularly beautiful stretch of bracken tinged to autumn gold or quaint, low cottages standing ruggedly alone. But I was content to be driven over the miles of moorland and marvel at their vastness, their utter detachment.

Edwina shifted a foot and the car slipped smoothly into a lower gear.

About half a mile ahead at the bottom of a gentle incline, a huddle of houses nestled snugly in the lap of a hollow with the square, squat tower of a church seeming to stand guard.

"There we are, then. Slaidbeck," Edwina nodded. "Look—to the right of the church—standing alone."

She pointed to a white cottage in the distance.

"That's Keeper's"

"Keepers?"

"Keeper's Cottage, my home. A gamekeeper once lived there, hence the name."

"It's quite a way out of the village, isn't it?" I hesitated dubiously.

"Only about a mile."

I smiled. It all fitted. It was so like Edwina to find some tiny, half-hidden village then choose to live apart from it.

"Aren't you lonely, sometimes?"

"No. You're never lonely in Slaidbeck. They don't let you be. You belong; you've got to."

I didn't understand, but Edwina lapsed into herself

again and it wasn't until we were seated in soft, low armchairs before a fire that crackled pine logs in a wide inglenook that she seemed to want to talk.

"Tell me about Johnny."

The question was terse as it was sudden.

I placed my tea-cup carefully on the small table at my side, studying the intricate tracing on the thin china for a long time before I spoke.

"Like I told you," I said. "He's missing."

Edwina looked at me without speaking and for a little while the tension of the past few days gripped me again.

"And . . .?" she prompted.

I shrugged, lowering my eyes to the floor.

"Well—the more I think about it, the more I just don't believe it."

"What do you mean, Kathy? *Why* don't you believe it?"

I hesitated again, searching for the right words, strangely reluctant now the time had come, to talk to Edwina. But I told her again about Johnny: of the man who had come to tell me about the abandoned Land-Rover and the coat and the wallet. It came out in jerked and incoherent sentences and all the time Edwina sat unmoving and listened without interruption.

"So you see," I finished, "I can't believe it—any of it. Johnny can take care of himself. It's just not like him to go missing."

"No," Edwina agreed, thoughtfully.

"That's why I'm afraid," I rushed on. "There's something very wrong; I can sense it. It's a feeling so strong that I can't control it. I can't explain it, either."

For a moment Edwina stared into the fire as though trying to draw an answer from the flames.

"It's going to be all right, Kathy."

She lifted her eyes to mine.

"I promise you it will be all right," she whispered, gently.

Then she jumped to her feet.

"I need a drink. Want one?"

I shook my head. Quite suddenly there was a tension about Edwina that I hadn't seen before and I felt ashamed that I had added my worries to hers, for I was almost sure something was troubling her.

"Is anything wrong?" I asked.

"Wrong? No! Of course not. Why should anything be wrong?"

"I don't know. I get the feeling that something is worrying you."

"Well, it isn't," she returned, flatly.

It was foolish of me, I know. Edwina had flashed me the red light and I was stupid enough to ignore it.

"Don't you feel lonely, sometimes?" I persisted. "I mean, you're not married, or anything, and there's no one for you to share your troubles with. You're talented, Edwina, and attractive. You'd make a good wife—"

"Stop it, Kathy!"

I felt the colour rush to my cheeks. I was blundering in where I wasn't wanted.

"Sorry," I said, lamely. "It's only that I'm fond of you. I'd like you to be happy."

She turned and looked at me for a moment.

"Yes, I'd like that too—don't think I wouldn't—but the man in my life isn't available, Kathy."

"He's married?"

It was a relief at least to know what could be the cause of Edwina's tension.

She nodded.

"Then couldn't she—his wife, I mean . . . Well, hasn't he asked her to let him go?"

"Leave it!"

Edwina's words cut like a whiplash, but still I rushed on.

"But if they're not happy together . . .?"

Edwina flung round to face me, her eyes snapping anger.

"I said, *leave it*, Kathy!"

Then she closed her eyes tightly, fighting for self-control, her fingers tense round the stem of the glass she held. It seemed that any moment it would shatter in her hands. Then she took a deep breath and smiled bleakly.

"Sorry, lovey," she shrugged. "Only don't mention it again, uh?"

She shrugged her shoulders and began to gather the tea things together.

I felt a sickening wash of shame at my own self-pity. I had inflicted myself on Edwina and burdened her with my troubles. She had listened to me with sympathy and understanding whilst all the time she too must have been desperately unhappy.

"I'm sorry—truly I am," I said again, trying to make amends. "Let me help you with the dinner?"

"Okay. The casserole should be about ready, anyway. Come and talk to me whilst I see to the vegetables."

Then she smiled.

"Mind if we eat off trays tonight, Kathy?"

The storm was over. Edwina was herself again.

There were no more small silences that night, no guarded answers to implied questions. We sat, toes tucked beneath us, by the red brick ingle and talked of everything except those things we should have talked about. But with heavy velvet curtains shutting out the winter night and soft-shaded lamplight mellowing the white, uneven walls and casting warm shadows, I felt the tension slowly slipping from me. Here, encircled by thick old walls, my worries seemed to have receded into less sinister proportions and the animal instinct of danger unseen did not prick at my nostrils as it had done in the London flat. I tried not to think of Johnny, save to wish him well; tried to forget our differences and the high-pitched whistling that had warned of the coming of another angry scene.

Edwina talked with enthusiasm about her business, but for all that I sensed that there was still a reserve about her. She seemed strangely reluctant, too, to speak about Johnny. Was she, unknowingly perhaps, censuring me for wasting a happiness that was being denied to her? Edwina would not have watched unprotesting as I had done whilst her marriage crumbled about her. But I could not tell her the whole truth of the life Johnny and I had lived together. I could not even try to tell her about those watching eyes or the small knot of fear that twisted inside me as I waited for some new fury to break about me. Edwina could not know how the whistling of a love song . . .

I shook myself mentally. I would not think of it. I was safe, now. Tomorrow would be a new day. Perhaps tomorrow the sun would shine a little; perhaps there would be news from London.

Edwina sprang suddenly to her feet.

"I need a nightcap. Like one, Kathy?"

I shook my head as she poured whisky then splashed soda into it. It worried me a little that she seemed almost to need the comfort of alcohol. I could never remember her drinking at all, in the past.

"Fattening, lovey. That small glass is full of nasty little calories that zoom immediately to the hips," she once teased.

She seemed to be smoking heavily, too — but then, it was over three years since we had last met. So much, I knew only too well, could happen in three years.

"Ready for bed?"

I nodded and picked up my handbag, switching out lights as Edwina placed the guard over the fire.

"I'm taking the day off tomorrow in your honour," she

said as she followed me up the twisting staircase. "I'll show you the countryside and we'll see if we can't get some roses into your cheeks."

I kicked off my shoes and curled my toes into the thick white pile of the carpet. Edwina turned back the bedcover and switched off the electric blanket.

"Do you still like to sleep with the curtains drawn back?"

I nodded, happy she had remembered.

Outside, the moonlight tipped the hills with silver, glanced on the stark winter outlines of trees and cast strange blue shadows. It was so beautiful, so utterly peaceful that silly little tears pricked my eyes.

Briefly Edwina's lips brushed my cheek.

"See you in the morning, then."

"Edwina?"

I wanted to say so much to her; to thank her for taking me on and my worries; for the comfort her strength gave to me, but for the first time in my life I couldn't. Something indefinable had happened; some strange web of uncertainty hung between us.

"Nothing," I shrugged. "Just — well, thank you."

A little smile flickered for an instant on her lips.

"Good-night, Kathy," she whispered.

I lay for a time, snug and warm, my eyes taking in the dim outlines of the moonlit room. Here, as on everything, was the mark of Edwina's good taste. She had taken the neglected old cottage and stamped her personality on it, blending the old with the new as only she knew how, losing nothing of the old-world charm to modern plumbing and lighting. I sighed contentedly and thumped the rose-coloured pillows. I was sure that tomorrow everything would start to come right. Tomorrow, I decided, I would tell Edwina about the money and about the bank manager and what he had said regarding the painting. Perhaps, too, I'd tell her the whole truth about me and Johnny; about his silences and my inability to cope—about our dead love.

I was drowsy, now, and my body felt light and relaxed. For a fleeting moment I thought I was imagining it, that in my contentment I was warning myself against the feeling of complacency that cocooned me.

It came to me through a haze of drowsiness and I jerked my eyes wide open and willed myself awake, shaking my head to clear the bad dream. For a while, only the shuddering of my breathing broke the stillness, then I became aware of the textured pile of the sheets in my clenched hands and knew I was not asleep.

Desperately I groped for the light at my bedside, fumbling with useless fingers to find the switch. A soft light flooded the room reassuringly and I filled my lungs with gulps of air. I could hear the thudding of my heart, feel the racing of small, frightened pulses in every part of my body.

Then it came again, raping the calm of the lovely night, its melody unmistakable, each note clear and menacing on the cold air.

I'll take you home again, Kathleen,
Across the ocean wild and wide . . .

The blankets felt soft and real in my hands. My blue dressing-gown lay where I had left it at the foot of the bed. I was not asleep, I had not dreamed it. Outside in the vast night, someone was whistling.

I ran my tongue round lips dry and stiff with fear then flung back the bedclothes and hurled my body towards the door.

"Edwina!"

She was leaving the bathroom and we collided on the landing.

"Come and listen!"

I clutched blindly for her hands.

"Come and listen, Edwina. Outside. In the garden!"

"Kathy! For heaven's sake . . ."

She shook off my trembling hands and grasped my shoulders firmly. Desperately I struggled to free myself but her grip held me.

"Stop it! Do you hear me, Kathleen? *Stop it!*"

Her voice was harsh.

She thinks I'm having a nightmare, I thought wildly. She thinks I'm hysterical and she's going to slap me!

I fought to control the cold panic that possessed me, drawing air deep into my lungs and letting it out slowly.

"Edwina, please listen to me."

I tried to speak calmly.

"I'm not dreaming or sleep-walking or anything. I'm all right, now, but please, *please* come into my bedroom. Please *listen?*"

Grasping her hand, I begged her with my eyes. Mystified, she followed me to the window.

"Listen," I demanded.

For a little while the ticking of the tiny bedside clock filled the room as we stood, waiting, our eyes on the black void of glass.

Then it came again, deliberate and unmistakable. I fumbled with the catch and flung open the window. The whistling filled the room and echoed all around me, piercing my brain, screaming inside my head. It went on and on until I wanted to shout:

"Stop it! Stop it! Go away!"

Then suddenly it ended.

"You heard it?" I whispered. "It was Johnny. He's out there."

With an exclamation of annoyance Edwina slammed shut the window, angrily swishing the curtains together as if to blot out the night and all it contained. She turned, her eyes searching for mine and for a moment we faced each other, unspeaking.

"You heard it?" I pleaded.

"Sit down, Kathy."

Edwina guided me towards the bed.

"Now, tell me all about it."

"It was Johnny! Don't you see, Edwina—he's not missing. He's down there, in the garden, whistling."

Edwina did not speak.

"You believe me, don't you? You heard it, like I did!"

"Kathy, love."

She shook her head and dropped her eyes, her fingers fidgeting with the folds of her dressing-gown.

"I'm sorry, Kathy, but I don't understand you."

"You don't understand?"

How could she *not* understand? There had been no mistaking it.

She looked at me pityingly.

"Come downstairs to the fire. I'll make you something to help you sleep."

She spoke coaxingly as if she were trying to humour a truculent child.

"I don't want to go downstairs."

"Very well," Edwina shrugged, sitting down beside me again.

"Look," I tried to speak steadily and calmly. "Johnny is outside. He's in the garden. That was his whistle, Edwina, the tune he always whistled."

Shakily I hummed a few bars of the melody.

"He was always whistling it, Edwina, and when he did there was trouble. That's why I'm afraid. Something is wrong—very wrong."

"Kathy . . ."

Edwina's voice trailed off. She was still looking at me

31

with that half-pitying expression in her eyes. It stung me to rebellion.

"You don't believe me! You think I imagined it, don't you? *Don't you?*" I insisted, shrilly.

"No, lovey, I don't."

"You heard it, didn't you? You must have heard it!"

She did not speak or shift her eyes from mine. I felt a surge of panic. Angrily I jumped to my feet.

"Edwina, tell me, please."

My voice betrayed the tears that threatened.

"Someone was whistling in the garden. It was Johnny and you heard him, like I did. *You heard him*, Edwina!"

Still her eyes did not waver.

"There's no one out there," she said, emphasising every word.

I stared at her. I couldn't speak.

"You were dreaming, Kathy. *You* didn't hear it and *I* didn't hear it. You imagined it, I tell you!"

I didn't believe I had heard Edwina aright. How could she say that when she'd heard it herself?

The gaze that met the anxious searching of my eyes was compassionate. It was the look people reserved for small children and dumb creatures or those who didn't know any better. People who were . . .

I put the thought from me. I wasn't mad. I had heard that whistling. It was as simple as that but it was useless to try to reason further with Edwina. Besides, I needed time to think, to get things straight in my mind. You couldn't better Edwina when her mind was made up—I knew that from the past. It was like kicking at a wall with bare feet. It got you nowhere; it was a relief to stop.

So I submitted to her cosseting, to the hot-water bottle she placed at my feet, to the plumping of pillows and the glass of brandy she placed in my hand. I drank it, protesting as it burned my throat and snatched at my breath.

"Things will be all right in the morning, you'll see," she soothed. "Now go to sleep, and no more nightmares."

But it wasn't a nightmare, I silently fretted. *Oh, Edwina, why couldn't you hear it too?*

I don't know when sleep finally came to me, but I awoke feeling anxious and depressed. Edwina was standing by the bed with a tray of tea.

"It's a lovely morning," she smiled. "Crisp and bright and just right for a long walk. Hope you brought warm clothes with you."

She made no reference to the incident of last night and I knew she had already dismissed it from her mind.

Well, I decided, if that was the way she wanted it, that was the way it would have to be. And perhaps I really had imagined the whole thing. Could it have been a dream?

I knew with dull certainty it had not, yet as always I took the least line of resistance.

"Hmm. Thick and warm and," I added, looking at the exquisite housecoat she was wearing, "very sensible."

"We'll go down to the village and do the shopping, then we'll take the rest of the day off," Edwina pronounced after breakfast.

"Let me help you with the dishes," I offered.

I felt lethargic and dull-witted, the result, I knew, of lack of sleep.

"No need, lovey. It's Mrs Hatburn's day today."

"You've got a daily?"

"A once-a-weekly," Edwina corrected. "I was lucky to get her. Very particular who she does for is Mrs H. Think it was my new-fangled kitchen as she calls it, that did the trick."

She took down the pad and pencil that hung on the kitchen wall.

"I'll write out my list while you get your bath."

Obediently, I accepted my dismissal.

The hot water and an extravagant slurp of Edwina's bath oil refreshed me and helped lift the unhappy cloud that still hung over me. I was able to coax myself as I lay in the scented blue water that perhaps I was making just a little too much of the whole incident. After all, it needn't have been Johnny who whistled last night. It could have been a shepherd, perhaps, or a poacher. There could have been some quite innocent explanation for it all, except that there were no sheep anywhere near Edwina's back garden and poachers didn't usually advertise their presence by whistling.

And if it had all been so innocent, nagged the little imp of doubt that was never very far away, why had Edwina denied hearing it?

With an exclamation of annoyance I reached for a warm towel.

"Today," I told myself, firmly, "is a new day. Yesterday doesn't matter — it's over and done with.

I caught sight of my reflection in the mirrored wall and smiled back at it. I looked better when I smiled. The hot water had relaxed me and brought a faint flush to my cheeks and the shadows that smudged my eyes seemed a little less noticeable. If only, I thought, I had a little of Edwina's flair; the tiniest part of her self-assurance, her vivid personality. I sighed and shrugged away the wish then thought better of it, smiling again at the uncertain woman who stood pink-towelled before me.

"Bathroom's empty," I called down to Edwina as I ran, barefooted, to dress.

The sky was a rare, clear blue as we walked quickly

down the lane and the first frost of winter had silvered the fields and the tops of the greystone walls. The faint wind that blew from the hills pinched my cheeks and I threw back my shoulders against the cold, matching my step to Edwina's.

"Shouldn't you be working?" I asked. "I mean, can you really spare the time away from your business?"

I felt a stab of guilt about the way I had inflicted myself upon the pattern of her well-ordered life.

"No, I shouldn't and yes, I can. After all," Edwina shrugged, "I have a first-class staff and they're well able to run things without too much interference from me. I don't intend to get premature wrinkles by worrying unnecessarily."

I felt the colour flame in my cheeks and I wondered if the remark was intended for me. Did I worry too much and was that worry mostly a figment of my imagination?

With the exhilarating air catching at my breath and the gaunt hills reaching up all around us into the clear sky, I could almost convince myself it was.

"I'm a fool, aren't I—worrying about everything—hearing things?"

"Hmm." Edwina smiled indulgently.

"I mean, if it had been Johnny last night in the garden, he wouldn't just disappear into thin air again, would he? People don't do things like that, do they?"

"I wouldn't have thought so."

"Then what am I getting so het up about?"

Edwina smiled again, a faraway, non-committal quirking of her lips, and the thought struck me that in some ways she was very like Johnny. I wouldn't care, I thought, to stand in the path of her single-minded ambition.

"Look, Kathy, at the bend in the lane. That's the Tithe Barn. It's as old as Methuselah, they say, and quite unique."

I reined-in my thoughts, following Edwina's pointing finger. But I didn't look at the timbered barn, or if I did I didn't see it.

I saw instead the man who lounged indolently against the age-old stones, saw the straight black hair with its slightly receding hairline and the near-arrogance of his unhurried movements as he calmly turned his back and walked on.

I was glad we were too far away to see the expression in the eyes I knew were black and deep and hard; grateful that Edwina was at my side.

I hissed his name between teeth clenched tight with terror.

"Johnny!"

THREE

I closed my eyes then opened them again. Rooted to the spot, I grasped Edwina's arm.

"Kathy? Kathy—what is it . . .?"

I shook my head, incapable of speech. I just stood there and stared at the spot at which I had last seen him, nodding my head in the direction of the barn, pointing a finger that trembled uncontrollably.

"Johnny." I mouthed.

"Kathy—now look here . . ."

Stung by Edwina's disbelief, I found my voice again. It came in an unfamiliar croak.

"It was Johnny! He was standing there, by the barn. You saw him, Edwina. You *must* have seen him!"

"There's no one by the barn."

"But you couldn't miss him. You pointed at the barn and he was there. I saw him—why didn't *you?*"

"I tell you there is *no one by the barn.*"

She spoke slowly, emphasising every word.

"No, Edwina; not now. He's gone now, but he *was* there. He was wearing a red sweater; a red polo-neck sweater. You couldn't miss a colour like that."

"Kathy!" Edwina's voice was harsh. "Stop acting like an idiot. First the whistling, now this!"

The tingling that crawled under my scalp shivered down my back and I felt a wave of naked panic wash over me, Edwina didn't believe me! I had seen Johnny but she had seen no one. I had seen him as plainly as the weathered beams by which he stood and even at a distance

I'd recognised every movement of the careless, swaggering walk.

"I want to go back, Edwina," I said, my voice low-pitched now with terror. "I won't walk past that barn. Johnny was standing there, I tell you. I saw him and I saw him walk away. If you didn't see him then you're as blind as a bat or —"

I covered my face with my hands, shutting out the blank oval of disbelief that was Edwina's face.

"Or what, Kathy?"

For a while I couldn't speak, for the effort of fighting for control of my cold, trembling body was almost too much. Then, between the gasping sobs, I whispered, almost as if I didn't want her to hear:

"Either you are blind and deaf, Edwina," I faltered, unwilling to say the words that screamed inside my head. ". . . either that, or I am slowly and surely going out of my mind!"

"Oh, Kathy. Kathy, love," Edwina's voice was gentler now. "Look — I'm sorry if I sounded harsh. I didn't mean to — you know I didn't."

She placed her arm round my shoulders. "It was just that — well, you did give me a bit of a turn."

She laughed shakily and I had the fleeting impression that even she had lost a little of her composure.

"Let's go back, shall we? We'll go home and make a cup of tea."

Her placating tone irritated me. She was doing it again, I fumed inwardly. She was treating me like a child. But my mouth felt dry, still, and my hands were shaking inside the pockets of my coat.

"Yes please," I whispered. "I'd like that."

My whole body ached as we walked slowly back to Keeper's, neither of us speaking. I wanted to reason with Edwina, try to convince her I was right. I had seen the barn clearly, the walls around it, the moss-covered roof. And a man was standing there; a man who wore a bright red sweater. I watched him turn and walk away towards the village. I couldn't have imagined all that. Edwina *must* have seen Johnny.

But she didn't know him, I reasoned. Perhaps I had seen some other man who from a distance resembled Johnny. Could I have been mistaken? Was I in such an emotional state of mind that I was ready to believe that any dark-haired male I saw looked like my husband? I didn't know, but of one thing I was quite sure. Some man had stood by the barn yet Edwina insisted that no one had been there. *Why?*

"I'm not going out of my tiny mind you know," I said, later.

I was feeling a little calmer, helped no doubt by a glass of Edwina's brandy.

I picked up my tea-cup and managed a very weak grin.

"Many more shocks and I'll be getting to like the taste of that stuff."

I nodded towards the glass at my side, laughing as I did so. But it was a forced laugh, nervous and slightly hysterical.

"Purely medicinal." Edwina reached for the decanter. "Want another?"

I shook my head.

"No thanks. And next time do me a favour. Give me sal volatile!"

"There won't be a next time, Kathy. You've had it rough—first the baby, then Johnny. Of course you're upset. It'll come all right, just you see," she smiled.

"You think so, Edwina? You're not just trying—"

My voice trailed off. I didn't want to plead for

reassurance and hear Edwina's gently coaxing reply. Impatiently, I jumped to my feet.

"I'm sorry. I'm a fool and a nuisance into the bargain. I'm acting like a spoiled brat and you haven't done your shopping."

"It doesn't matter," she shrugged. "I can ring the shop; they'll deliver anything I need."

As if to prevent any further argument, she picked up the telephone.

I was glad she did, because deep inside me I was still afraid. I didn't want to go to the village or walk past the barn. I just dare not risk seeing the man — seeing *Johnny* — again.

"I can put him off if you don't feel up to it, Kathy."

"Uh?" I looked up, startled. "Sorry, Edwina, I was miles away."

"I know you were. About half a mile away, to be exact, worrying about a man in a red sweater."

She clicked her tongue impatiently. "I said that if you wanted, I'd put Mike off, tonight."

"Oh, you mean the friend who was coming for a meal? No, don't do that," I hastened. "I'd like to meet him, really I would."

Edwina had obviously made her plans and would be looking forward to the evening. It would have been churlish of me to refuse and anything would be better than sitting with twanging nerves, waiting to misinterpret the banging of a door or the hoot of an owl in the quiet of the night.

"Really," I insisted, "I'd like it very much. Who is Mike?"

"Michael Carter. You'll like our Doctor Mike, Kathy."

"I will?"

"Hmm. The most eligible bachelor for miles around."

"Oh? So he's not married, then?"

Edwina shot me a warning glance. I hadn't been very tactful and she had understood my implication only too well.

"No, Kathy; Mike isn't married."

I had the grace to blush and the sense, this time, to let the matter rest. It was obvious the doctor held no special interest for Edwina and her private life was no business of mine. If and when Edwina wanted me to know who her lover was, she would tell me in her own time.

There was a tension between us again.

"My hair's a mess," I said.

I didn't care very much how it looked, but at least the remark served to break the silence.

"Yes, it is," Edwina agreed in her forthright way. "Look, I'll give you a hand with it, if you like. Let's wash it in rainwater—maybe put some life back into it."

She looked at me critically.

"You know, Kathy, I always envied your lovely hair when we were at school. It's just criminal, the way you've let it go."

She grinned to take the edge off her forthright outburst and I grinned back, glad at least for something to take my mind off Johnny.

Gradually, the tension eased away and it seemed for a little time that we were at school again, laughing and indulging in girl-talk, preparing for the end-of-term dance.

"There now."

Edwina speared the last of the large, fat rollers. "You'll feel a million dollars tonight. And for heaven's sake, Kathy, throw away that pink lipstick!"

She rummaged in a drawer.

"Here. Try this one. It's exactly your colour."

She was right as she always was. The tawny-coral shade

41

seemed to light up my face. I smiled through the mirror at Edwina's reflection.

"It looks good."

Briefly her eyes held mine and for a little while it seemed that the years between had truly rolled away and we would maybe be able to exchange confidences again as we had done so often in the past. But Edwina merely placed her hand lightly on my shoulder and said:

"And you look good, Kathy, when you remember to smile a little."

She left me then and went downstairs and I heard her talking to Mrs Hatburn who was working in the kitchen. I sat for a moment, chin on hands, dispassionately gazing at the face before me in the mirror.

Edwina was right. My hair had once been the envy of my schoolfriends. They'd even thought I was quite pretty, I remembered. But there was a tenseness about me now; a tightness around my mouth — a furrow between my brows that would soon be permanently etched there if I didn't stop brooding.

I had always been a worrier, even as a child. Perhaps it had been born of timidity and shyness. I hadn't one aggressive bone in my body, truth known. Anyone could trample over me and I'd just apologise nicely for getting in their way.

Not so with Edwina. Nothing and no one had been allowed to stand in Edwina's way. She wouldn't have lain awake half sick with fright because she heard a whistle in the dark; Edwina wouldn't have been driven to near-hysteria by the distant sight of a man in a red sweater.

I was being foolish, I told myself firmly. I was making mountains out of molehills. It could have been anybody whistling out there and there was no law against the wearing of red polo-neck sweaters, either.

"You're being a fool, Kathleen Parr," I asserted firmly to

the pale-faced woman in the mirror. "Nothing, not *any-thing*, is ever as bad as it seems. Have any of those things you've worried so much about in the past ever happened? Be honest now; *have they?*"

I wrinkled my nose. Of course they hadn't, or at least, not many of them.

Tonight, I resolved, I would try to enjoy myself, for Edwina's sake if not for my own and tomorrow I would telephone London and ask for news of Johnny. Whatever I believed I had heard and seen, that at least I must do.

Picking up the lipstick, I outlined my mouth again and smiled. Then I tied the bright green chiffon scarf Edwina had left me around my head and got finally to my feet.

"I will try," I asserted. "I really *will* try."

"Phew! Well, that's everything ready!"

Edwina threw herself with cat-like grace into an armchair.

"Be a darling, Kathy—I need a drink."

Frowning a little, I poured a meagre tot and splashed it well with soda.

"There you are."

I handed her the glass.

"One hundred calories—at least!"

"Cat!" she grinned at me. "Bottoms up!"

I sighed with exasperation. Despite her directness I loved Edwina dearly. We were opposites and that, I supposed, was why we got along so well together.

I kicked off my shoes and settled myself by the hearth, tucking my toes beneath me, nestling into the luxurious softness of the chair. The afternoon had passed uneventfully and now, with soft lights glowing and logs blazing in the wide hearth, I felt a rare contentment inside me. Edwina had been right. Everything would work out, given time.

"You look good, Kathy."

I blushed with pleasure. Praise from Edwina was praise indeed. But I'd had to admit as I made up my face and brushed out my hair that it had been a long time since I had taken such pains with my appearance.

My hair hung soft and loose on my shoulders and the dark shadows that still lay beneath my eyes were hardly visible beneath a little careful shading. Now, in the lamplight, I stole a glance in the mirror and felt that perhaps Edwina was right. I looked a different person.

But if I looked good, Edwina was quite superb. Her simple dress of soft wool fell full-skirted to her feet and a broad belt nipped her tiny waist making it look even more slender. For a moment she looked fragile and vulnerable and my heart went out to her. I felt a small stirring of anger against the man who had taken her love when he had no right to do so. I hoped with all my heart she would not be hurt, for sometimes I sensed that beneath the brittle, hard-headed business woman she had become, Edwina yearned for a husband and children of her own. It was strange, I thought sadly, that we both seemed to have made a bit of a mess of things.

Edwina jumped to her feet.

"There's Mike's car," she called over her shoulder as she went to open the door.

Michael Carter was late but Edwina seemed not to mind. She seemed in fact to expect it.

"Evening surgery crowded and an accident at Dark Fell farm," he explained, briefly and ruefully.

"Come and meet my guest," Edwina said, handing him a drink. "Kathleen Parr—Kathy—Mike Carter."

The hand that took mine was warm and strong.

"Kathy?" He smiled down into my eyes. "Suits you."

I smiled back. I felt immediately at ease with the tall, fair man.

"Be a darling and look after Mike whilst I dish-up the supper."

Edwina left us alone but I felt no shyness as I usually did with strangers, and as we talked I studied Michael Carter closely.

He looked tired but his hands were relaxed on the arms of the chair. They were gentle hands, as were his eyes. For some silly, inexplicable reason I was glad his eyes were blue—the bright, steely-blue of a sailor's eyes or those of a countryman. His hair was in obvious need of cutting and from time to time he flicked away the lock that fell over his forehead as if he too was well aware of the fact.

We talked as if he and I had been friends for a long time. It seemed strange that he didn't mention Johnny or ask me anything about London.

We spoke instead about Slaidbeck and his contentment to be an overworked country doctor, on call for twenty-four hours a day. He told me about the far-flung farmsteads that could become isolated for days after a heavy snowfall and of the hills, aloof and treacherous.

"I hope Edwina warned you not to walk alone on the hills, Kathy. They can be very beautiful and tempting but there are boggy stretches with tracks across them that only the sheep and shepherds know."

"I think people who have such majestic countryside to look out upon are very lucky. I think the hills are romantic," I defended.

"Romantic and savage—remember that. You've got to learn to read the weather before you can be on equal terms with the hills and moors. The mists can come down without warning—especially in winter."

"I'll remember," I smiled, knowing it was almost certain I would never venture far alone, especially since Johnny was . . .

I snapped off my thoughts. I would be happy tonight. I

wouldn't think about anything at all, except how good it was to laugh a little.

I insisted, when we had eaten, that I should wash the supper dishes.

"Bless you, lovey," Edwina almost purred. "You can't know how I dislike disposing of the remains of a meal."

She settled herself comfortably by the fire and blew me an exaggerated kiss of thanks.

I hummed almost happily beneath my breath and tied a small, frilly apron around my waist.

Edwina's kitchen was a delight; a clever blending of old and new. A brass chain-lamp hung from a beam, copper ladles and ages-old cooking spoons decorated the walls, and beside an alcove lined with old-fashioned storage jars stood a rocking-chair. It was a real Granny kitchen and I loved it.

With my hands firmly grasping the tray of glass and china I pushed the light-switch with my shoulder.

"Clever girl," I whispered triumphantly as the carefully concealed strip-lighting flickered and glared into brightness.

Then suddenly the smile of contentment hardened on my lips and the familiar feeling of fear was back again. I looked away from the window then looked quickly back.

"Edwina," I whispered, my throat constricted with sudden shock.

I stood, so frozen with fear that for a moment in time I couldn't move but stared like a small frightened animal at the face of a man that peered through the window.

My hands shook uncontrollably and the tray tilted. There was a shattering crash as glass and china scattered and splintered on the floor.

"Edwina!" I screamed and the tray fell with a clatter from my nerveless fingers as I turned and ran.

Mike took the full force of my flight as we collided in the kitchen doorway. He glanced briefly at my face.

"What is it, Kathy?"

I pointed a trembling finger at the window.

"A man!" I gasped. "A man, looking in at me!"

With a couple of strides that seemed like superhuman leaps, Mike reached the door and wrenched it open. I heard his footsteps as they ran down the garden path.

Edwina was by my side now and I was sobbing uncontrollably.

"Don't tell me I was imagining it again. I wasn't, I tell you. I wasn't!"

Quickly Edwina laid an arm around my shoulders, placing herself between me and the window. I clung to her, my shoulders rising and falling with emotion as I gasped:

"Oh, Edwina, you've got to believe me this time. There *was* a man. I saw him!"

"Look, lovey . . ."

Lost for words, she tried to lead me back to the normality of the sitting-room but I stood my ground, fighting for control of my shaking body. Edwina must believe me this time. She *must*!

"Please," I gulped. "Please believe me. There was a man in the garden. He stood at the window. He stood there and he stared and stared!"

"Kathy, tell me. What was he like, this man?"

"I don't know. I really don't know. But he stared and that's all I know for sure. But I *did* see him, Edwina."

I was spent now, emotionally and physically.

"Please, I'd like to sit down."

Gently Edwina led me back to the hearth and settled me, unresisting, into a chair.

"Here, drink this."

She wrapped my fingers round a glass.

"No!" I jerked. "No, I don't want it!"

She stood, the rejected brandy in her hand, and looked at me again with a pity that was becoming all too familiar.

I shook my head, wearily. Michael Carter would know now how stupid I was. I had liked him; I felt I could have trusted him. Now he too would churn out the old clichés of comfort and reassurance.

But would he? Mike was a doctor and he'd probably dealt with people like me before; people who screamed in uncontrolled panic because they thought they had seen something.

"Oh, Edwina."

I covered my face with my hands.

"What's to become of me?"

"Nothing, love. Nothing at all. We'll wait for Mike to come back before we start jumping to any silly conclusions."

"There *was* a man, Edwina."

The kitchen door slammed. Fearfully I raised my eyes to the doorway.

"There's Mike. Ask him. He'll tell you . . ."

Quizzically Edwina quirked an eyebrow.

"Well?" she demanded.

"Kathy was right," Mike replied. "There *was* someone. Dickie!"

"Dickie?"

I looked from one to the other, not understanding their obvious relief.

"Dickie Hatburn, Kathy. Mrs Hatburn's boy," Edwina explained.

"Boy? It wasn't a boy. It was a man."

"I know. Dickie *is* a man, but he's got the mind of a child. You see, for all his size and strength, he's still about six years old, mentally. Dickie wouldn't hurt you."

"But why was he hanging about in the dark?"

48

I was still unconvinced.

"Why was he looking through the window?"

"Perhaps he wanted to see you, Kathy. Maybe Mrs Hatburn told him you were here visiting. He's got the curiosity of a child. There's no harm in him, believe me, love. No harm at all."

I looked questioningly at Mike Carter and he nodded reassuringly.

"I'm sorry," was all I could say, taking a long, shuddering breath.

Sorry I had broken Edwina's beautiful china; that I had made a fool of myself again and that Michael Carter had witnessed my childish display. And I was sad because my peace of mind had been so short-lived. Suddenly it became important that Mike should know all about me.

"I've been seeing things, Doctor," I said, dully, "didn't Edwina tell you? Is that why she asked you here tonight—to look me over professionally?"

"Kathy, that's not true and you know it!" Edwina retorted hotly. Then turning to Mike she explained:

"Kathy's had a rough time, lately. She lost her baby and now her husband is believed missing. It's only natural she should be a little jumpy."

"Oh dear. Poor little Kathy."

Gently Mike took my wrist and laid his fingers on my pulse.

A little jumpy! But you haven't told Mike everything, have you, Edwina? You forgot about the whistling and you forgot we'd seen Johnny. Only you said you hadn't seen him, Edwina, when you had!

"Not too bad," Mike pronounced. "Just a little erratic. I'll give you something to make you sleep if you'd like, Kathy. You'll be fine again in the morning."

I thanked him. I was too emotionally drained to protest. For a little while I had lulled myself into a false sense of security. I had willed myself into believing that there was some perfectly simple explanation for what had happened. But I hadn't imagined Dickie Hatburn and I knew now I hadn't imagined the whistling or the man who stood by the barn—the man who could have seen Johnny.

Mike took two tablets from a container in his bag.

"Here you are, Kathy. One now and one at bedtime."

He picked up his coat. I thought he looked a little embarrassed.

"Think I'll try to get an early night," he said to Edwina. "I'll look in tomorrow if Kathy would like me to."

I shook my head. I'd caused enough upset already.

"Thanks, Mike, but no. I'll be fine. Like Edwina said, I'm a bit jumpy." I smiled my thanks. "Really, I'll be fine."

"Right. Well—see you again soon, perhaps?"

"Okay. See you," Edwina said as she rose to see him to the door.

I was sweeping up the litter of broken glass and china when Edwina returned. I tried to say how sorry I was.

"Forget it," she shrugged. "They're all replaceable."

I turned on the hot tap and squirted liquid soap into the sink.

"Well," I quipped. "This is where I came in."

My attempt at a joke fell flat. Neither of us felt much like laughing.

I awoke in the morning feeling rested. The tablets Mike gave me had done their work and I had slept deeply and without dreaming.

"You look fine," said Edwina.

She was dressed in outdoor clothes and I knew that soon she would be setting out to visit one or another of her boutiques.

"I don't like leaving you here but there's a couple of manufacturers I must see. Look, Kathy, why don't you come along with me? You'd enjoy it and I'd like it better if you did."

I smiled and shook my head.

"I'm not dressed and besides, I feel nice and relaxed this morning. I'll be fine, Edwina — honestly."

"Would you like me to look in at the surgery on my way out and ask Mike to call?"

"No thanks; I'm okay, truly I am. I'll have a lazy morning and have something ready for you to eat when you get back."

"If you're sure . . .?" she hesitated, picking up her handbag.

I smiled reassurance.

"See you about half-past two, then," Edwina replied, doubtfully.

She seemed reluctant to leave me, but I smiled as I waved from the window then watched her car disappear from sight.

The coffee in the pot was still hot and I poured a cup and buttered a slice of toast.

Mike had mentioned that his morning surgery was at nine-thirty. If I hurried, I reasoned, I could still make it in time. The breakfast table could wait until I returned.

On awakening, I had made up my mind, suddenly and with absolute certainty, to go and talk to Michael Carter. I didn't know why. I only knew I needed help and I was sure that if Mike was able, he would give it to me. I needed to talk to someone who was unbiased and properly equipped, too, to deal with people like me.

I had thought, when I came to Keeper's Cottage, that Edwina would help me, but I had been wrong. Edwina had problems of her own and beneath her blasé exterior I knew that for some reason she was jumpy as a kitten. I had to try to sort things out for myself. Edwina, it seemed, had problems enough of her own.

I remembered later, as I pulled on my coat, that I had intended to phone London for news of Johnny.

I picked up the receiver and then replaced it. I knew what the answer to my call would be. There would be no news to give me. Johnny was missing and no one would find him until he wanted to be found. It came as no surprise that I had at last stumbled on the truth of the matter.

I bit my lip nervously and made for the front door. Then I froze, my hand on the knob.

Someone was walking up the path.

But it would be the postman, of course. I fixed my eyes on the flap of the letterbox.

The slow, shuffling footsteps came nearer and I felt my breath catch in my throat as I waited. There were no letters and the footsteps stopped. Someone was standing on the doorstep and I waited for the knock that did not come.

The palms of my hands were wet with nervous sweat and I thought wildly that I might slip quietly through the hall and out of the back door — down the garden and across the fields . . .

Then suddenly the door vibrated as if someone was kicking on it with a heavy boot.

My heart thudded painfully. I felt sick with terror and my one thought was to hide and wait until it was safe to leave the house. Surely, if I didn't answer they'd go away? But I'd had enough of that. I was tired of cringing at my own shadow, of imagining unseen dangers, of acting like some spineless creature. It had to stop or before long I would have reached the point of no return and there would be no help for me. I had to open that door — *now!*

With every pulse in my body beating a small tattoo of fear and every instinct I possessed urging me to run, I flung open the door.

FOUR

For an awful moment it seemed I was suspended in frozen terror, then my eyes began to focus once more and I found I could breathe again without its hurting me. A tall young man stood on the doorstep. His cheeks glowed red with cold and there was a hesitant smile on his lips. His hands were cupped gently round a bird with a wing that hung loose and bloodstained. It was strange that in one panic-stricken second my eyes should see so detailed a picture; stranger still that I should instantly sense he meant me no harm. There was something familiar about the shock of curly hair, the broadness of his shoulders.

"Dickie!" I whispered. "It's Dickie Hatburn, isn't it?"

I let go a long, shuddering breath.

"Hullo, Miss."

He looked down shyly at his shuffling feet.

"I'm sorry I kicked at your door . . ."

He held out his cradled hands as if in explanation.

"I found this bird in Miss Howarth's garden. It's hurt its wing and it can't fly."

"What is it?"

"It's a thrush . . ."

His face registered surprise at grown-up ignorance.

". . . a missel-thrush."

"Oh, I see. Well, I'm not very good about birds, Dickie, and I'm afraid I don't know how to make its wing better."

The speckle-breasted bird lay still within his hands, its eyes closed. Poor frightened little creature. Its tiny heart

53

would be beating with instinctive terror; it would feel trapped and helpless. I knew that feeling so well.

"I know how to make it better, Miss. I know what to do with it."

"Do you, Dickie? Can you really mend a broken wing?"

"It's wing isn't broken; it's just hurt and bleeding. I think one of the wild cats must have done it. I'll look after it and I'll let it go as soon as it's better. But it can't fly and the cats will get it again if I don't take it home."

I realised he was asking me if he could take the bird. He had found it in Edwina's garden and thought, child-like, that it belonged to her.

"Miss Howarth isn't in this morning, but I'm sure she will be very pleased if you could make the bird better. Of course you can take it home," I smiled. "You'll be kind to it, won't you?"

He laughed, then.

"Of course I will. I like birds. I won't hurt it—promise."

I knew at once that he wouldn't. This gentle young man wouldn't hurt anything. How silly I had been, last night. I remembered the broken glass and china and felt a wave of shame. But I had been startled. Too many strange things had happened; I couldn't really be blamed for reacting as I had done.

I was glad I had decided to talk to Michael Carter. If anyone could help me sort myself out, I was sure it would be he.

I was feeling calmer now and just a little pleased with myself for opening the door. It had been quite brave of me, really. Anybody could have been standing there.

I smiled tremulously.

"Yes, I know you'll take care of it, Dickie. Look—I'm going down to the village and I don't know the way. Would you let me walk along with you?"

The words came out glibly and I didn't feel very proud

of my lies for, if I were honest, I was apprehensive about walking alone to the village. I didn't want to pass the tithe barn. In spite of my brief show of bravery, I was still in such a state of tension that I would willingly use anybody as a prop, even simple Dickie Hatburn.

I went quickly and locked the back door, buttoning up my coat as I did so, trying to ignore my burning cheeks. Well, I thought grimly, it was going to be a lot different from now on. Things had come to a pretty pass when the sound of footsteps on a garden path could reduce me to a mass of jelly. Something was very wrong, of that I was quite certain, but surely I didn't have to go half out of my mind to prove it?

Afraid? Of course I was afraid, but if I could learn to control my fears and act, outwardly at least, like a rational human being, I'd be nearer to getting at the truth.

I smiled at Dickie.

"Shall we go, then?"

We strode down the lane unspeaking. Dickie walked carefully, his eyes not leaving the little bird for a second and all the time making small hushing sounds of comfort.

I was glad of his concentration. I didn't want to talk for I was still on edge, my eyes sliding to either side of me, my back tingling from the sheer effort of refusing to let myself turn and look behind me. I stared fixedly ahead as we rounded the bend in the lane, my eyes alert for the slightest movement in the vicinity of the old stone building. I heard my sharp, uneven breathing and desperately willed my feet to move and my heart to stop its thudding.

The barn, when we reached it, appeared to be just as Edwina had described it yesterday—old and quaint and nothing more sinister. A huddle of sheep sheltered beside it and a wild pigeon, its feathers fluffed out against the cold

55

wind, perched forlornly on the time-mossed roof. There was nothing, I told myself, nothing at all, to get upset about.

And then, just as I began to relax a little, when I had almost convinced myself it was all right, that I was being foolish and over-imaginative, Dickie began to hum softly to himself. It seemed almost as if he too felt Johnny's presence and had remembered, then, the soft, plaintive melody:

I'll take you home again, Kathleen . . .

My mouth went suddenly dry and the familiar feeling of fear possessed me again. Unable to speak, I looked sideways at the man-child who walked alongside me. There was no malice in his face; just compassion and innocence and he hummed the tune softly to the injured bird as if in sympathy.

Why should he pick that tune, I reasoned, and at that exact time and in that exact place? Could he, like me, have heard it in the night? Could it, I thought with a surge of hope, have been Dickie I heard whistling that night and not Johnny?

"Do you think the little bird likes your song, Dickie?" I whispered, my lips stiff.

"Uh?"

He turned and looked at me, not understanding.

"Can you whistle, Dickie? Can you whistle loudly; louder than the birds do?"

"Course I can," he shrugged.

"Who taught you that tune—the one you were humming just now? Did your mother teach it to you or did you hear someone whistling it? *Did you*, Dickie?"

"I don't know."

Suddenly his face became an irritating blank.

"I didn't hear anybody whistling it," he countered. "I—I made it up myself!"

Then he set his mouth stubbornly and strode ahead of

me, anger in his walk, his head tilted at defiance. I had almost to run to catch him up.

"Look, Dickie," I urged, more gently, "don't be cross with me. I only wondered if—"

"I'm not talking to you any more," he retorted with childlike petulance, "and I don't tell secrets."

"Ooh. Have you a secret? I like secrets. Tell me, Dickie? I wouldn't split—honest."

But he just looked at me, grinning tantalisingly, and I knew it would be useless to coax him further.

"All right," I retorted with exaggerated nonchalance, "I don't care, anyway . . ."

He laughed then; a teasing, playful laugh as if the whole thing was a big joke and it didn't matter at all that he had suddenly hummed the one tune in the whole world I didn't want to hear.

We didn't speak again until we reached the village, and at the small store that was also the post office I stopped. I didn't know where Michael Carter held his surgery, but for some strange reason I didn't want to ask Dickie.

"I'm going to buy a stamp, now," I lied. Then I smiled. "Thank you for showing me the way to the village, Dickie. Will you let me know when the little bird gets better?"

"Yes, Miss," he said. "Yes, I will."

Then he turned and walked quickly away, leaving me strangely puzzled and, for all his innocence, not a little troubled.

Morning surgery, when I eventually found it, was almost over. Only one patient remained. I sat down, nodding a good morning.

Picking up a magazine that would have been of more interest to a farmer, I waited for the ringing of the bell that would tell me it was my turn to go in. I felt strangely uneasy when eventually I knocked on the door.

"Come in, please."

Mike's voice gave me reassurance.

"Kathy! But how nice."

He rose to his feet.

"Are you the last one in? I'll go and lock the outer door, if you are."

I nodded.

"We can go into the back room and have a coffee," he called over his shoulder.

"Look, Mike," I said awkwardly when we were settled, "this isn't a social call. I just wondered if you could spare me a few minutes of your time."

"Surely."

He poured boiling water into two mugs.

"How about a slice of Mrs Hatburn's fruit cake?"

"Please."

Suddenly, I felt hungry.

"Does Mrs Hatburn work for you too, Mike?"

He nodded. "She cleans the surgery every day and does my flat once a week. And she bakes pies and cakes for me."

"She must work very hard."

"Has to. Her husband was a regular soldier. He was killed in Korea just after Dickie was born."

"I met Dickie again this morning."

I told Mike about the thrush.

"Can he really mend its wing?"

"Dickie has an uncanny way with birds and animals," Mike nodded. "They seem to trust him."

"I shouldn't have been afraid of him. I was stupid last night, wasn't I?"

"Not really, Kathy. You had reason enough for acting as you did."

"I went into a blind panic again, this morning."

I studied the crumbs on my plate.

"Edwina was out and I heard someone walk up the path. It was only Dickie, but I didn't know that, of course. I just went cold with fear."

"But you *did* open the door?"

"Yes, eventually, and you can't know how relieved I was when I realised who it was."

"Who were you expecting, Kathy?"

"I don't really know." I shook my head. "I just expected trouble."

"Why? Why should you expect trouble?"

I shrugged, wishing now I were anywhere but sitting in Mike's surgery.

"Oh, it's a long story," I prevaricated, "and you are busy, Mike."

"I've two routine calls this morning, that's all."

I didn't speak.

"What is it, Kathy?"

Prompted by the kindness in his voice I whispered:

"Last night, when I told you I was imagining things, I meant it. I've been hearing things and seeing things."

"Tell me."

So I told him, and as I did I realised the utter futility of getting over to him—to anybody—my sense of foreboding, the inexplicable smell of fear, the feel of imminent danger. But strangely Mike seemed to understand.

"Edwina said you've had a rough time lately. Your husband is missing—you lost your baby. It's natural you should wonder what more can happen."

It was strange, I mused, how little I had thought about the death of my baby son. I had pushed it purposefully into the dark corners of my mind, remembering only that his death had been my fault—mine and Johnny's. We had quarrelled violently and that quarrel had caused our child to be stillborn. It was all I ever remembered about it. If only I could have mourned; cried until every unhappy tear

59

had washed my guilt away. But perhaps, I thought, I hadn't suffered enough yet.

I said:

"Losing a baby is like living through a nightmare, Mike. I don't think I will ever come to terms with it."

"You will," Mike soothed. "When your husband is home safely and all this is behind you, you'll forget—or at least, the grief will go."

My husband. Johnny. I wondered yet again where we had gone wrong. It had all been so wonderful at first, the loving and belonging; being together. Perhaps we should never have married.

When had all the bitterness started? Had our mad happiness ended the night I told Johnny I was pregnant? Had he felt shackled after our marriage? The moods had started, then. It began to be a relief, almost, each time he packed his kit and left for another job at another Middle Eastern oilfield. And we had quarrelled a lot each time he came home. That had been when the baby died . . .

"Kathy?"

Mike's voice cut through my thoughts.

"Sorry," I blundered. "I was thinking about . . ."

I shrugged. I didn't want to talk about it.

"You were thinking about your husband, Kathy. Say it," he smiled gently. "Talking about a thing often helps. And this time next week, you know, you may be together again and wondering why you were so unhappy."

I looked up quickly.

"Johnny's being missing doesn't make me unhappy. It makes me afraid."

The words were out even before I knew it. But I couldn't have stopped them for someone else had spoken those words. Some other woman who stood dispassionately behind me, who intercepted my thoughts and said the things I didn't have the courage to say. That woman—my other self—knew in her heart what I dare not admit. She knew it mattered to me that Mike should not think I was grieving for Johnny.

"I'm sorry," I said. "I shouldn't have said that."

No, Kathleen? mocked my other self. *But you thought it, didn't you?*

It shocked me to admit that I had, that I was being callous and cruel. I must never again allow myself to feel this way. I must try to find pity for Johnny. He could be lost still, and ill, fighting to survive. I must wish him well, I urged; hope that soon he would be found.

But how do you find a man who isn't lost?

I raised my eyes and looked at Mike. He was sitting quietly, waiting for me to regain control of myself, willing me to go on.

"I'm sorry," I whispered again.

"What are you trying to say, Kathy?"

"I'm trying to tell you—"

I dropped my eyes again, watching my fingers twitch nervously in my lap.

"I'm trying to say that I don't believe Johnny is missing—at least that he's not in any danger. I'm the one who's in danger, Mike. Don't ask me why. I don't know why. But I can sense it. You see, I know Johnny."

"You *know* him?"

"I can't explain it," I nodded. "I can only say that if Johnny were in any real danger I would feel it and I don't. I don't feel anything."

"Have you told Edwina what you are telling me?"

"Most of it. But she doesn't know about Johnny's moods. She doesn't know what it was like when the whistling started, waiting for the lash of his tongue. Edwina has never seen Johnny's eyes when—"

I clasped my hands tightly together, squeezing my eyelids against threatening tears, unable to trust myself to go on.

61

I'm making a fool of myself again, I thought. This way, nobody's going to listen to me, let alone believe me. But Mike's voice was kind when he said:

"Sorry, Kathy. I hadn't realised how things were."

He pushed a tissue into my hand.

"Come on, then, let it go. Have a good cry."

He placed his arm around my shoulders.

"That's better," he urged as sobs shook my body. "You know, tears aren't just for onion-peeling."

I managed a watery smile, gulping back my sobs.

"What must you think of me, Mike?"

"I think you are upset and suffering from delayed shock. I believe you are afraid, too."

"You do? You don't think I was imagining things — hearing the whistling, seeing Johnny?"

"I believe you heard and saw *something*, Kathy. Would it help if I had a talk with Edwina?"

"No!"

My reply was harsh and positive. "Not Edwina, Mike. I don't want Edwina to know I've been to see you, either."

I shrugged, resignedly.

"Besides, she doesn't believe me. She thinks I'm going mad."

"Surely not? Don't you think you are being just a little bit unfair?"

So that was that. I reached for my gloves. I'd told Mike and he didn't believe me either. I was being unfair to Edwina and I'd made a fool of myself into the bargain.

"I'm sorry I've wasted your time, Mike," I said, more stiffly than I'd intended. "Thanks for the coffee and sympathy!"

I stood for a moment, hesitating. Mike did not attempt to show me out. Instead, he remained seated in his chair.

"Steady on," he smiled slowly. "I'm quite certain Edwina

doesn't think you are in the least bit mad. You are a bit jumpy, though."

He took his pipe from his pocket.

"Now truly, I'm really not too busy this morning. Suppose we try to get to the bottom of this, eh?"

I relaxed a little.

"We'll not get to the bottom of anything if you persist in humouring me."

"I don't humour my patients."

Mike struck a match and held it to his pipe.

"I take it you are my patient, Kathy?"

"I don't know. Am I?"

I wondered what he was trying to say. That I liked him was becoming increasingly obvious to me. Was it also obvious to Mike? Was he placing me in the same category as those bored, neurotic women who liked to unburden to their doctors? Was he putting me firmly in my place, right at the start of things? Surely he couldn't think I had any other interest in him? It would be a long time before I would wholly trust another man, let alone become emotionally entangled with him.

The woman inside me laughed derisively. I was protesting too much, and she knew it.

"Do medical ethics allow one's friends to become one's patients," I asked, primly.

"Certainly. Just so long as they remain only friends."

Then he laughed.

"Think I'd be hard put to it to make a crust in Slaidbeck if that were the case. Most people around here are friends as well as patients."

"I'd want it to be on a business footing, Mike."

"I don't take private patients, Kathy, but I'll give you a card though, to fill in — a sort of temporary transfer whilst you are here."

He rummaged in a filing cabinet.

"Might be a good idea if I got in touch with your regular doctor. Would you mind if I did?"

"I suppose not, but why should you? You don't have to go to any trouble, Mike. I just felt a bit strung-up, that was all. I mean, after last night's performance . . ."

"Forget about last night. What I am more concerned with are the circumstances that caused last night's performance, as you call it. That's why I'd like to contact your doctor."

I shrugged. "It's all right by me if you really think it's necessary."

"I do."

"Right."

I took out my diary, and opening it at the front page, passed it to him.

"That's fine."

Mike wrote down the name and telephone number beside it.

"I think a phone call might be quicker."

He smiled and laid down his pen.

"Now, suppose you make us another cup of coffee whilst I find you a couple of tablets?"

"Sure," I said, trying to be more matter-of-fact about the whole thing than I felt.

Why hadn't Edwina noticed how attractive Mike Carter was, I wondered as I rinsed the mugs under the tap. I couldn't understand why she should let herself fall in love with a married man when Mike would have been so much better for her. They'd have made such an attractive couple, I thought. Where were Edwina's eyes, I sighed.

"Penny? For that long-suffering sigh, I mean."

I felt my face flush.

"I was thinking about Edwina."

Mike grinned.

64

"Don't sigh for Edwina, Kathy. Edwina is quite capable of looking after herself."

"I know. She's efficient and self-sufficient and it makes me want to take myself in hand when I'm with her."

"Well, don't. She's Edwina; you're you. You are all right as you are."

Blushingly I thanked him, wishing I hadn't mumbled. Edwina wouldn't have mumbled.

"Here you are."

Mike pointed to the tablets in the palm of his hand. "The small ones are mild sedatives and the larger ones will help you sleep. There's enough for two days."

"Oh, dear — is that all you trust me with?"

I quirked down the corners of my mouth with mock severity. "Think I shall swallow them all at once or something?"

"Please yourself," he grinned back. "The lot of them together would only make you very sleepy and probably a bit sick."

I wanted to hug Mike. He wasn't humouring me. He was treating me like a normal human being — well, almost normal.

Feeling much happier, I placed the small envelope containing the tablets in my handbag then got to my feet.

"I really must go. I want to do some housework and get a meal ready for Edwina."

I held out my hand.

"Thanks for listening, Mike. It's helped a lot, really it has."

"See you tomorrow, then, for another chat, if you can manage to get down without Edwina knowing."

He frowned.

"Although why she shouldn't know, I really can't imagine."

"Please, Mike. I'd rather she didn't know."

I felt disloyal to Edwina. She had been kind to me, and it struck me that if Mike had insisted on an explanation I couldn't have given him one. I didn't know why something inside me wanted to be so secretive.

"Suit yourself."

Mike rose to his feet and walked with me to the front door.

"'Bye, Kathy, and remember, if things get rough, you know where to find me."

I tried to decide as I walked back to Keeper's Cottage just what my visit to Michael Carter's surgery had achieved. That I felt better for talking to him was obvious and he had seemed in no way dismayed by my emotional behaviour. I wondered why he wanted to get in touch with my doctor in London, but perhaps, I shrugged, it was the usual thing to do. I didn't know a lot about doctors, really. I'd once been pretty fit. The last time I had seen mine was after the baby died.

Poor little scrap. It had been my fault; everything I tried to do, I made a mess of. But things would be different, soon.

I straightened my shoulders. Mike would help me sort myself out. Perhaps, if I could pull myself together; if I could learn to be calm and a little less afraid of life, it might be easier to make a go of things with Johnny if he came back to me. Then I shook my head as if to cancel the negative thought. Johnny would come back, there was nothing more sure. And when he came back, what then?

I closed my eyes for an instant. I wanted him to be safe, but I knew now, with absolute certainty, that the love I once felt for him had died.

What in this world, I thought miserably, can be deader than dead love?

A tractor pulling a cart behind it crawled noisily up the lane ahead of me, churning up the grassy edges with its huge wheels. With a surge of relief I realised I could walk behind it, unseen and unheard, until I had safely passed the barn. I hurried to catch up with it. Being brave, I thought with apprehension, wasn't going to be easy. It wasn't going to be easy at all . . .

Edwina returned sooner than I expected.

"You're early!" I exclaimed.

"I wanted to get back quickly—"

"But you shouldn't have rushed."

Her concern touched me.

"I've been all right," I protested.

"No, I meant . . ."

She stopped, embarrassed. Then she shrugged her shoulders as if what she had been about to say was not important any more.

"Did anyone call?" she asked, off-handedly.

"Call?"

"The phone, Kathy. Did anyone ring?"

"No. Well, if you'd said you were expecting a call I'd have stayed in."

The words slipped out before I knew it.

"Stayed in? You've been out?"

"Just down to the village and back. I—I felt like some fresh air," I faltered.

"Oh." Edwina lit a cigarette. "Well, it doesn't matter. I just thought—"

"Look, I'm sorry, Edwina. I didn't realise it was important."

"It *wasn't*. I just asked if there had been any calls. Don't make a thing of it, Kathy."

Then she smiled. "Anyway, they'll ring back if it was important, won't they?"

"I suppose so. *If* anyone rang."

Edwina kicked off her shoes and sank into a chair.

"Forget it, lovey, and pour me a sherry, uh?"

I did as she asked, thoughtfully.

'Forget it,' she had said. But she had made just a little too much of it for me to do that. I should have known, of course, who the call would have been from. *He* hadn't called and now Edwina was disappointed. I sighed. If only she would tell me about the man.

"And you needn't sigh so dramatically. It's only one small sherry before lunch."

Edwina wrinkled up her nose at me.

"And come to think of it, what are we eating, and when?"

"Steak and salad," I answered briefly. "It's under the grill and ready in five minutes."

"Good. I'm hungry."

But Edwina's forced gaiety did not deceive me. Something about that phone call didn't ring true. Either she was very disappointed or, strange though it seemed, very relieved.

Suddenly I realised that for once it was I who was being calm. Now it was Edwina who drew a little too deeply on her cigarette, who fidgeted in her chair, whose fingers twisted and untwisted in her lap.

"Dickie Hatburn called this morning."

"Dickie?" Edwina looked up sharply as though she had not heard what I said. Then she laughed.

"Oh, Dickie . . ."

I nodded.

"What on earth did *he* want?"

"He found a thrush in the garden. Its wing was hurt. He asked if he could take it home."

"Oh," Edwina nodded absently, dismissing the subject from further discussion.

She spoke little as we ate our meal. Indeed, for one who had only a short time ago declared her hunger, she seemed surprisingly without appetite.

"I've brought you a present," she said, quite suddenly. "Here . . ."

She handed me her car keys.

"A present for me? But, Edwina, you shouldn't have."

"All right then, I shouldn't have."

She smiled gaily at me, a little of her sombre mood disappearing. "But there's a box in the boot of the car, so you'd better go and get it."

I did as she asked, glad that whatever had troubled her on her return seemed to have placed, in Edwina's orderly way of things, into its proper perspective.

The box when I opened it revealed a most beautiful dress of a russet shade that was instantly right for me. It looked exactly what it was; understated to the point of simplicity and extravagantly expensive.

"Edwina; it's beautiful."

I held it to me, feeling its sensuous softness.

"Oh, it's absolutely beautiful!"

Impulsively I leaned towards her and kissed her cheek.

"Oh, you're so kind. Why did you do it?"

I felt a slight stiffening of her body at my touch. She showed no emotion, as if the giving of so expensive a gift was a slight embarrassment to her. She turned her head away from me.

"A peace offering, perhaps . . ."

I didn't reply, for even if I had been supposed to hear the enigmatic words, there was nothing I could have said. I didn't bear any grudge because she had spoken to me sharply. Edwina should not have needed to square her conscience with a peace offering.

But I didn't want to bring the matter up again. Mike Carter would, I was sure, help me over my bad patch.

Edwina had done more than enough for me already. It was I, really, who was the debtor.

Carefully I draped the dress over a chair.

"Sit by the fire and have a cigarette whilst I do the dishes," was all I could think of to say.

The fleeting November sun dwindled into a fierce red ball in a grey afternoon sky and still we sat, comfortably talking of trivialities. Between us the telephone seemed to sit like an unexploded bomb, for whenever there was a lull in the conversation, it seemed that our eyes were drawn involuntarily to it. I half wished it would jangle into life and that *he*, whoever he was, would put an end to Edwina's waiting. But the tantalising thing stayed strangely silent for the remainder of the evening.

Poor Edwina, I thought; waiting like a schoolgirl in the throes of first-love for a telephone call that didn't come.

I wished with all my heart as I lay in bed that night that there was something I could do to help. But there was nothing to be done, I knew, but wait.

I closed my eyes but sleep did not come at once. I thought about Michael Carter who had been kind to me and Dickie Hatburn who had carried an injured bird in his great, gentle hands and hummed a tune as he walked. Dickie, who had a secret.

FIVE

The rear lights of Edwina's car had hardly disappeared into the early-morning gloom when the telephone rang.

It was ironic that after she had spent the better part of yesterday waiting for its ring, it should choose to end its silent sulking almost the minute Edwina left the cottage.

For a moment the sudden strident clamour knocked me off balance and I was reluctant to answer it. Perversely I had no wish to speak to Edwina's lover, for I felt an instinctive dislike towards him. I had always thought that love should be a thing of great happiness between two people. Edwina's love, it seemed, was not like this.

My hand reached for the receiver and I drew in a deep breath.

"Yes?"

"Kathy—I thought you'd never answer!"

"Mike! It's you . . ."

"Who else were you expecting?"

"I don't know—nobody, I suppose," I replied, laughing with relief.

Could it be only my imagination or had the dull, ordinary morning suddenly become very special?

"Kathy, I'll be making a call in your direction in about half an hour. Are you alone? Can you rustle up a cup of coffee?"

"Sure. That would be fine, and Edwina's just left."

I felt guilty and deceitful.

"Is it important, Mike?"

"Not really. It's only that your doctor told me—"

71

"My doctor? You've phoned him already? What did he say?"

"Nothing to get upset about. He said that when he last saw you, you were in good physical shape — a healthy young female . . ."

He hesitated perceptively.

". . . but it'll keep until after I've called in at Dark Fell farm."

"You're sure, Mike?"

"Of course I'm sure. Stop worrying!"

There was a little teasing laugh in his voice and it comforted me.

"All right," I said, dubiously. "See you?"

I was standing by the window when Mike arrived and as he backed his car onto the wide grass verge outside the gate I opened the front door.

"I'm glad you've come," I greeted him, grateful for his warm, safe presence.

He smiled in return then unwound his scarf, throwing it on the settee.

"Right! How about that drink?"

I set cups and the coffee-pot on a low table. My hand trembled as I poured and the scalding liquid slopped into the saucer.

I tried to make a joke of it.

"I'm dithering again . . ."

"Why, Kathy?"

"I don't know. Perhaps I'm a bit bothered about what my doctor — what Doctor Martin told you."

"Why should you be? What do you imagine he said?"

"That I'm neurotic, I suppose," I shrugged, concentrating desperately on the pouring of the coffee, hoping my forced nonchalance was making an impression.

"After all, I imagine things, Mike — hear things."

I handed him the cup and he stirred it thoughtfully before replying.

"Well, he didn't. In fact, he wasn't very forthcoming at all, which is understandable. But what he did say gave me no cause to worry—at least, not about you, Kathy."

"About whom, then?"

Mike took a pipe and tobacco from his pocket. He didn't look at me.

"Your doctor said you were in good physical shape, all things considered."

"Things like what?"

"That you had not long been confined when he last saw you and that you had—"

"That I'd lost my baby?"

"Yes, Kathy."

"I see. Then if there was no cause to worry unduly about me, who *was* he worried about?"

Mike attended to the lighting of his pipe with emphasised care.

"I don't think," he said between puffs, "he was actually worried about anybody, but from what he implied, I gathered that all wasn't well with you."

"What reason should Doctor Martin have for saying that?"

Mike shifted uneasily.

"Well, put it this way—I got the impression that it wasn't only the loss of your baby you had to contend with."

"I see. I had other things to worry about, you mean?"

"Yes," Mike supplied flatly. "Your husband."

"You mean, he told you he thought there was something wrong with Johnny? How wrong?" I demanded, the familiar tingling shivering down my back again. "Was Johnny physically sick, or was it something else?"

"Look, Kathy," Mike shrugged, "I couldn't glean a great deal—well, you know how it is? Your doctor wouldn't be

73

able to say a lot over the phone, would he? It was just that, rightly or wrongly, I got the impression that your husband didn't impress Doctor Martin very favourably, that's all."

I took a deep breath and hesitated a moment before going on. Now it was important—desperately important— that Mike should believe me. It seemed that Doctor Martin was on my side and to get myself into a state now wouldn't help at all.

"Look," I said, willing myself to be calm, "Don't you see now that it's not me—that I'm not the one who's going round the bend?"

"I never thought you were, Kathy. Not for a moment."

"Then what shall I do? Johnny isn't missing—at least he isn't now—he's here, in Slaidbeck. I've heard him whistling and seen him and so has Edwina, only she won't admit it!"

I took a deep breath and reached for the cigarette box.

"You don't need those."

Gently Mike took the box from my hand.

"All right, then. But tell me one thing, Mike. Why is Johnny trying to make me doubt my reason?"

"I don't know. Are you sure he is? Can you be absolutely certain it was your husband you heard whistling? Was there a man in a red sweater?"

I set my lips stubbornly in an effort to speak slowly and calmly.

"I'm sure I heard Johnny whistle," I whispered, "and there *was* a man in a red sweater standing by the barn. He was a long way off, but I'd swear it was my husband."

"Even though Edwina didn't see a man at all?"

"Even though Edwina didn't see him. And how could she have been so certain, anyway? She doesn't know Johnny."

I fixed Mike with a long, steady stare.

"Tell me something? Why should Edwina act so strangely? What reason could she have?"

"I can't tell you, Kathy. I can't even begin to guess at it, but if she heard the whistling and saw the man by the barn, why should she deny it?"

"I don't know. Maybe she saw and heard as clearly as I did. Perhaps she was telling little white lies to calm me down—to humour me. They do humour you, don't they, Mike, if they think you're mad?"

Mike was silent. Deliberately he spooned a piece of milk-skin from the top of his coffee. It was as if he was playing for time, trying to order his thoughts. Then he looked at me and his eyes were very gentle.

"Kathy, *you are not going mad*," he said slowly. "I do know a bit about these things, you know."

He set down his cup, then took my hands firmly in his own.

"Now look at me. Do you understand what I said?"

"Yes, I understand," I whispered, "but—"

"No *buts*. Just let's establish the basics, then go on from there."

"All right. I'm not going mad. Now what?"

Mike released my hands and placed them gently in my lap.

"Now you can have that cigarette, if you really want it."

"No thanks." I shook my head.

"Good girl," Mike smiled approvingly. "Let's get down to business, then. When did your jumpiness start?"

"I don't know," I shrugged. "I've always been timid, ever since I can remember. Boarding school would have been hell for me if it hadn't been for Edwina. They have a term for people like me, I believe: *lacking moral fibre*."

Mike grinned. "One thing you don't suffer from is an inflated ego."

I smiled, in spite of myself. I felt better. My hands had stopped trembling, now.

"Seriously, though, I was always ready to lean on Edwina

75

when we were kids together. I always took the least line of resistance."

"And your marriage, Kathy? Was your husband really cruel?"

"Yes, he was, but it was very subtly done and of course I felt it more because he knew I was easily frightened. It wouldn't have succeeded for one moment if he'd been married to someone like Edwina."

"Perhaps not."

Mike leaned back in his chair.

"Maybe a touch of the Edwina's might have done your husband the world of good. Perhaps you should try it yourself, when this muddle gets sorted out."

"No, Mike." I shook my head firmly. "No matter what happens, I shall not go back to Johnny. That much I am sure about."

"Poor little Kathy. Was it so very bad?"

I nodded.

"It was like living with two different men. One minute it was all wonderful—the next minute I'd not know what had hit me. And it got worse and worse until we couldn't speak to each other . . . It was his eyes, Mike. His eyes frightened me more than anything."

"Could there have been a reason for these sudden changes of mood? Did he drink?"

"Yes, but not a lot."

I jumped to my feet and stood by the window, my back to Mike.

"Oh, I feel so disloyal. I shouldn't be talking like this, should I?"

"Yes, if it helps us to get to the bottom of things," Mike returned, mildly. "I *am* your doctor, however temporary."

"All right," I nodded. "What else do you want to know?"

"Did your husband smoke? Could he have been taking drugs?"

I shook my head.

"No, Mike, not drugs, and he only smoked on occasion. He looked after himself—you know, visits to a gymnasium when he came home on leave—running round the park. He wouldn't have taken drugs."

"No family history of fits—epilepsy, or anything?"

"Not that I know about. But I never met his family. His parents were both killed in the London blitz."

"No worry about money?"

"I don't think so. He had a good job."

"No gambling?"

"I'd have thought not, but he could have, though, without my knowing. Latterly, he went out a lot when he was home on leave. He never said where he was going. Oh," I added, just to cover everything, "and he wasn't keeping a mistress, either. I'd have known it, I'm sure of *that*."

"Yet you honestly think that you have some reason to fear your husband?"

"Yes, Mike, I do. Discount the whistling and the barn incident if you like. After all, you've only got my word for that and I've no proof to offer. But Doctor Martin could have been right; something *could* have been worrying Johnny."

"Like what, Kathy?"

"Like fourteen-thousand pounds."

"Johnny owed fourteen-thousand pounds?"

"No," I shrugged, then walked slowly back to the chair. Mike wouldn't believe me, I knew it. No matter what I said, it would all sound too fantastic. I lifted my head and said as calmly as I could:

"I found a deposit-account statement for fourteen thousand pounds."

"And you're worried about *that*?"

I closed my eyes then. I'd known all along, I thought

77

hopelessly that it would sound mad. No woman should be worried about the acquisition of so much money. But for all that I willed my voice to be steady.

"Wouldn't you worry if you were me? If your husband hated you so much it showed, wouldn't you get the jitters if he went missing and suddenly you found you were rich? The money had been put in *my* name, Mike. I can show you the statement if you want. At least I've got proof of *that!*"

"I believe you, Kathy. But is that what has made you suspicious and frightened? Why?"

"Because Johnny was quite often in the red at the bank and because all that money came from the sale of a painting, the bank manager told me. Only we never had a painting to sell."

"And . . .?"

I looked up and saw there was no laughter or doubt now in Mike's eyes, so I told him everything, right from the beginning. About finding the key and opening the desk; about the bank statement so obviously left there and about the bank manager's so delicately phrased suspicions.

"So don't you feel it all sounds very wrong, Mike?" I finished. "When you think of everything that has happened, wouldn't you be afraid too, if you were me?"

"Yes, I think I might," Mike acknowledged slowly. "I wish you'd told me about the money before. You think your husband came by it — well, dishonestly — don't you?"

My cheeks flamed as I nodded.

"But there's something else, Mike. I've got to be fair. Remember yesterday I told you I walked down to the village with Dickie Hatburn?"

Mike nodded encouragement.

"Well, just as we got to the barn, Dickie started humming —"

"And it was the tune Johnny whistled? *I'll take you home again . . .?*" Mike supplied, promptly.

"Yes, it was."

"So you're thinking now that it could have been Dickie you heard whistling the night you first arrived in Slaidbeck?"

"Yes," I nodded. "Either that or Dickie had heard the whistling too and picked up the tune unconsciously. Dickie is always roaming about the fields. He could have been out that night and heard it. It was cold and crisp with a near full moon; a lovely night for Dickie to be out. He could have heard Johnny . . ."

Mike rubbed the back of his neck then smiled at me ruefully.

"I see what you mean," he admitted as he got to his feet, "and I think you did the right thing in coming here to Edwina."

I handed him his scarf and he wound it slowly around his neck.

"Look, Kathy, are you absolutely sure you won't let me have a word with Edwina?"

I shook my head vehemently.

"No, Mike. Edwina has done enough for me already. This is my problem now. Just so long as you think I'm not in danger of losing my reason, I can manage. It's about time I grew up and faced facts, isn't it?"

"But there must be something I can do to help you sort this thing out, Kathy. I'd like to try."

"No, Mike." I shook my head positively. "You've been very kind. You've helped more than you know. You've given me back my sanity and now I've got to take myself in hand; change my thinking; change my ways."

Mike picked up his bag.

"Don't change too much, Kathy."

He smiled, briefly.

"I'll keep in touch," was all he said as he walked towards the door.

"Thanks," I whispered. "Thanks a lot."

I wished with all my heart I could have said more, that there had been more between us, perhaps, than our professional relationship. But Mike was a friend and my doctor, and that was all.

The comforting smell of his pipe tobacco hung on the air long after he had gone and it gave me the courage to pick up the telephone. Now I had to stand firmly on my own two feet. Edwina had given me shelter; Michael Carter had listened to my story and I was almost sure he believed it now. But above all, one thing was blessedly certain in my mind. *I was not losing my reason*—at least Mike had convinced me of that. It would be something I could cling to when things got bad; something to bolster my confidence on those days when my new-found courage faltered. Mike would be there if I needed help. The rest was up to me.

I dialled the number the Welfare Officer from Johnny's firm had given to me.

"This is Kathleen Parr speaking," I said in a voice that was clear and confident.

They told me there was no further news of Johnny and I listened to placating phrases of sympathy and hope. But beneath the tactful concern, I sensed that something was being held back.

"And there is nothing more to tell me?" I persisted.

There was the slightest hesitation on the other end of the line followed by an embarrassed cough.

"Well, perhaps you should know, Mrs Parr—and it could mean anything or nothing, so you mustn't get upset—your husband never reported to Abu Dhabi."

"He didn't get there *at all*?"

"I'm afraid not. They expected him two weeks ago. His kit arrived, but he did not."

"But he left for Abu Dhabi—"

"And turned up in Iran—or at least his coat and some of his personal possessions did. And of course, the car he had hired. It is very strange, Mrs Parr; very strange indeed. But you mustn't worry. We'll soon get to the bottom of things. There will be some simple explanation, no doubt . . ."

Some simple explanation.

I had heard those words before, but the only person who could provide that explanation was Johnny, and the answer to it all wouldn't be known until Johnny decided it should be. There was nothing more to be said and almost thankfully I replaced the receiver.

Why, I wondered, had my instinct warned me against telling what I knew to the man from Eastern Oil.

"Don't bother looking for him in Iran—he's here, in the North Riding of Yorkshire . . ."

No, they wouldn't have believed me. It had been a hard enough job convincing Mike. And Edwina still refused to be convinced. Best to have said nothing.

Absently, I picked up the coffee-pot, draining it into my cup, but the near-cold liquid tasted bitter. I set it aside and sank into a chair, resting my head on the soft, thick upholstery, willing myself to relax.

Carefully I carried my mind back, minutely delving into the unhappy past for hitherto forgotten details.

Now I felt no pity for myself; I felt it instead for Johnny. A man who could act as he was acting was deserving of my compassion. What else was left for me to feel for someone who could bring himself to such deceit? I felt my fingers clenching the arms of the chair and stretched them into relaxation again. I had to work things out dispassionately. It seemed that the man who was my husband—Johnny, who once I had loved, was sick. He was another being, a person who could try to fake his own death then play macabre games with my reason. That other Johnny was near at hand, had whistled his sinister warning in the dark.

I tilted my chin. I had to try to be brave. What was happening was almost too fantastic to be credible, yet it was happening and I knew I must hold on to myself with every ounce of my strength. I was on my own with nothing to cling to but the slender lifeline of friendship Mike had thrown to me.

Automatically I rose to my feet and picked up the tray. The first steps back to normality lay in doing ordinary, normal things like washing-up cups, making beds and dusting furniture.

I glanced at the little carriage-clock on the mantel. In a few more hours Edwina would be home again and Keeper's Cottage would seem less empty. Meantime, there was work to be done; things to occupy me so that I should not think too deeply about the past nor upset myself unnecessarily about things I couldn't control.

I wasn't going out of my mind—that fact in itself was reason enough for rejoicing. Now there was someone who believed in me, who didn't humour me or look at me with pity or exasperation or treat me like a hysterical child. Something was very wrong—oh, I'd known that all along, but I could try to get to grips with it now that I knew I was sane and normal as the next person. In his own good time Johnny would get in touch with me, I was sure of it, and when he did, I resolved, he would find a different Kathleen; one who would no longer allow herself to be browbeaten or bullied, and when he phoned, as I knew he would phone . . .

My thoughts ended abruptly. I stood suddenly still, my hands clenching tightly the tray I was holding. The phone was ringing now, cutting through my thoughts, noisily demanding attention. I had been thinking about Johnny and I had willed him to ring me, I thought wildly.

My mouth was dry again and my heart beat a little faster as I put the tray down carefully, not once taking my eyes away from the jangling white instrument.

I would be calm and speak slowly and Johnny would realise he had lost the power to make me afraid.

Reluctantly I reached for the receiver and it felt cool in my burning hand. I took in a deep breath then held it, knowing that if I let myself speak at once I should betray the tight rein on which I held my feelings. More confidently now, gently letting go my indrawn breath, I waited.

No one spoke. There was just a great empty void that screamed and echoed silence in my ear. For a moment I listened, straining to catch the slightest sound.

"Johnny?"

I could bear it no longer.

"Johnny? I know it's you. I've heard you and seen you. I saw you by the barn as you meant me to . . ."

Still there was no answering sound and my voice seemed to vibrate loudly round the empty room.

"Johnny?" I said again, my voice almost cracking with the effort I was making to stay calm and fake indifference.

"I know you're not missing and I know about the money, Johnny. You can't frighten me any more, do you hear me?"

There was a click, sharp and final, then the impersonal purring told me the line was dead again.

Frantically I tried to think of what I had said. Had I fooled him? Had I sounded brave or even a little bit aggressive? Had Johnny . . .?

But need it have been Johnny? Wouldn't Johnny have used a public telephone, and if he had, wouldn't I have heard the warning pips?

Puzzled, I bit on my lip, because now it was obvious that the call, whoever had made it, had come from a private telephone.

Had it been Johnny, then? Could it have been a wrong number?

But if that had been the case, I reasoned, the caller would surely have spoken — apologised and cleared the line at once. He — or she — wouldn't have held on unspeaking, listening to my impassioned attempt at bravery. Even Edwina's lover would have had the good manners to —

Of course! Oh, why hadn't I thought of him before? *He* had phoned. It had been *him*!

I laughed out loud with relief. Heavens, what a fool he would think me. But I didn't care. He could think what he liked!

I hadn't made a very good job of being brave. The moment I thought Johnny was on the other end of the line I had felt apprehension again. But I had made a start. There was still so much I didn't understand, so much to be explained, but Mike believed in me and was willing to help me all he could.

I wouldn't — I *couldn't* — let him down.

SIX

A little before five o'clock, Edwina staggered into the cottage with her arms clasped around a large box of groceries.

"Weekend supplies," she announced. "You know, Kathy, it's nice having you around."

I raised a quizzical eyebrow as I rinsed a colander of sprouts beneath the tap.

"You're such a domesticated little animal. Really, I didn't know you were such a good cook."

She sniffed appreciatively as she set the box on the kitchen table.

"It's a casserole from Wednesday's leftovers," I answered briefly.

"Well, I'm not having you slaving over a hot stove all weekend, Kathy. Tomorrow night we are going out. I want to show you the Old House."

"The Old House? Where is it?"

"The other side of Dark Fell. It's a lovely place—built about three hundred years ago. It's a sort of road-house now, but very select. French chef and dancing after dinner. Most people I know go there Saturday nights."

Most people? Would that include Edwina's lover? Would he be there, maybe even with his wife? Was she a woman both unknowing and unsuspecting? And when they were together in company, did this man and Edwina steal small, intimate glances? Did they exchange deceptively polite conversation; little ordinary-sounding phrases that conveyed sweet, secret meanings? Did Edwina and her man ever dance together and if they did, were they careful that it was neither too much to attract attention nor too little to invite comment? Was it all just a thrilling game to Edwina, a tilting at the tight little code of behaviour in that small, country community?

I dismissed the thought emphatically from my mind. Whoever this man was, Edwina loved him deeply, of that I was sure, and what happened between them should be no concern of mine in any way at all.

"Sounds nice," I breathed. "I'd love to go."

But for all my good intentions, I couldn't dismiss Edwina's problem from my mind. Was I judging her too harshly? Was my moral thinking prissy and outdated? Did Edwina's lover have a wife who was ill or mentally sick, perhaps? Was this man a decent type at heart, torn between his wife and Edwina; a man, maybe, whose circumstances resembled those of Jane Eyre's Mr Rochester? Did he have a wife who existed in a childlike oblivion in some discreet nursing-home? Edwina's lover might, for all I knew, be like any man one might meet; like Michael Carter, even.

Like Mike?

I shook my head. I was becoming fanciful and the lonely, desolate countryside was causing it, I tried to convince myself. Why, Slaidbeck was even set in Rochester country, wasn't it? Slaidbeck would have done justice even to *Wuthering Heights*. A city-dweller like myself could be forgiven for imagining such things in this tight little village, ringed round by gaunt black hills and fells that could be alien and dangerous.

But Mike was attractive, I told myself, and he was kind and gentle. Why, then, was he without a wife?

I threw back my head and gave a derisive little laugh. And it was genuine, too, for I was laughing at myself and my silly, dramatic thoughts. Edwina's lover had no sick wife tucked away and I knew it. Edwina would have told me so, had that been the case.

"What do people usually wear at the Old House?"

I forced myself to take an interest in what Edwina was saying.

"Oh, anything, really." She waved a hand vaguely. "Formal, informal — trouser suits. You must wear your new dress, Kathy. It'll be exactly right."

I glanced speculatively at Edwina. There was a restlessness about her again. Her movements were jerky, her eyes over-bright, and she was talking too much — too much, that was, for Edwina. But it didn't take the brain-power of a genius to work out what was troubling her.

"The phone rang," I said casually as I placed the pan on the cooker.

"Oh? Who was it?"

I didn't look at her. I didn't need to. The sharp anxiety in her voice told me all I needed to know.

"Couldn't say," I replied with studied unconcern. "He — or she — didn't speak. I suppose it must have been a wrong number," I lied glibly.

"Yes, of course. That's it — a wrong number . . ."

She sounded agitated and she wasn't troubling to disguise it.

"You're sure they didn't speak, or anything?"

"No. Whoever it was said nothing."

But *I* did, I thought, and he'll probably tell you all about it, Edwina, when next the two of you meet. He'll tell you about my tirade of nonsense concerning someone called Johnny.

"I thought it was Johnny," I said, hating myself for my deception.

"Johnny?"

Edwina's eyes jerked wide open.

"Yes," I said slowly, picking my words carefully. "I told him — oh, I don't know what I said. I was in a bit of a panic, I suppose," I shrugged.

"But do you really think it was Johnny?" Edwina persisted. "Don't you think it really *was* a wrong number?"

The anxiety in her voice was unmistakable, but for all that I felt a small thrill of triumph. She was worried, and the only explanation I could offer was that she had seen Johnny by the barn. For some reason she had chosen to deny it, but she *had* seen him, I exulted inside me, or why was she behaving so strangely? Either that, or she knew the true identity of the silent caller and was trying to sidetrack me.

But if Edwina really knew that, I reasoned, suddenly vaguely uncertain, then why was she so anxious? And there was no doubting it. Edwina was very anxious.

"Look," I said, remembering afresh my new-found resolve of the early morning, "Does it matter all that much who it was? If it had been so very important they'd have called again and they didn't," I smiled, "so why don't we forget it and have a sherry whilst we're waiting for supper?"

I unfastened the apron I was wearing and walked purposefully into the softly lit living-room, amazed at my own calm, realising with a kind of crazy elation that now it was I who was behaving rationally.

'Why don't we indeed?" Edwina echoed, her voice still brittle. "Let's sink the whole bottle," she laughed, pulling out the cork with a little plop. "Let's live dangerously!"

She filled two glasses and, passing one to me with a none-too-steady hand, raised her own in my direction.

"Men!" she said, shrugging her shoulders and pulling down the corners of her mouth in exaggerated derision.

"Rot their socks!" I replied unsmiling, lifting my glass in reply.

Then we both giggled hysterically as we had done so often

in our schooldays together, and some of the tension seemed to lift from Edwina.

But in spite of that, she ate little of the supper I had cooked and drank what I thought to be far too much. Her hands seemed to be perpetually nervous and her false gaiety continued throughout the evening until she abruptly announced:

"Thank heaven it's Saturday tomorrow. I'm nearly asleep."

"You'll not be going out tomorrow, Edwina?"

"I will not," she answered emphatically. "Tomorrow and Sunday we shall spend being thoroughly lazy, Kathy, but right now, I want more than anything to go to bed."

Her speech was a little slurred and the drinks she had taken seemed now to have made her a little dejected. Even in the soft-shaded lamplight, her face looked taut and pinched.

"Are you all right?" I asked, concern obvious in my voice.

"Yes, Kathy. Don't fuss."

I accepted the brusque reply without offence for clearly she was not all right.

"Look, love, why don't you go to bed? I'll bring you up a cup of tea, if you'd like," I coaxed.

"Thanks. That would be nice."

She rose slowly to her feet.

"I'll lock up and see to the fire, Edwina." I picked up her handbag and passed it to her. "Now off you go. I'll be up in five minutes."

For a moment she stood quite still, looking at me thoughtfully.

"You know," she said slowly, "I'm very fond of you. For all my funny ways, I really am fond of you. You do believe that, don't you, Kathy?"

I placed my arm around her shoulders.

"Yes, Edwina; I believe you," I smiled, "and I'm very fond of you, too. Now go to bed! You're nearly asleep on your feet!"

There was a defeated droop to her shoulders I had never seen before and it worried me, for it was so utterly foreign to her nature.

"You know," she mumbled wearily, "you're my oldest friend and I don't want you to be upset."

She turned, her hand on the door-latch.

"Truly, Kathy, I want you to be happy."

Her eyes looked into mine and they were anxious and sad. It seemed, almost, as if they were silently pleading for understanding.

"Bed!" I ordered firmly. "This very minute!"

She hesitated for a moment, then opened the door and walked unspeaking from the room, obedient as a child.

I watched her climb the stairs and wondered what had brought about the alarming change in her behaviour. She was suddenly so different to the Edwina I had known and thought I still knew.

"If *that man* is around when we go out tomorrow night," I whispered fiercely to the caddy as I spooned tea into the pot, "I swear I'll be rude to him. I don't care how many invalid wives he's got! I'll be downright rude!"

The distant ringing of the telephone awoke me and I blinked my eyes open. I must, I reasoned, have slept quite late, for the room was bright with morning light.

I groped with my feet for my slippers then shrugged my dressing-gown around my shoulders. If I didn't hurry Edwina would awaken and after last night's sad little performance, I wanted her to sleep as long as she could.

The ringing stopped as I reached the door of my bedroom and I waited, lest it should start again. And there was no point, I reasoned, in going back to bed, now.

"No, I wasn't asleep but why did you ring me here? I asked you to call me at work!"

It was Edwina's voice, low-pitched and nervous, and I knew I had been too late.

I stood quite still at the head of the staircase, something inside me telling me to wait as Edwina's words, clearer now, reached me.

"But I don't know if I can—it might be awkward . . ."

A pause, then:

"That's unfair! Of course I love you. You know I do!"

I was listening to something that was private and very personal. I knew I should turn round quietly and close the door of my bedroom, yet I did not.

"Please believe me?" Edwina's voice pleaded urgently, "I didn't think it would turn out like this!"

Poor Edwina. There was no doubting who was at the other end of the line. I backed carefully towards my bedroom door, praying silently that the creaking board on the landing wouldn't give me away. I didn't want to hear any more—indeed, I wished I had not heard so distinctly Edwina's anguished cry:

"No! No, I tell you! I won't have her hurt! Do you hear me? *You mustn't do anything to harm her!*"

Gratefully I reached the door and closed it gently behind me, my cheeks burning with indignation.

How could he, I thought? Not content with making Edwina unhappy, it seemed now that his wife was about to be made to suffer.

I won't have her hurt!

The words rang in my ears, still. It was obvious what they had been talking about and I was glad Edwina was trying to do what was right. One thing was certain, though. Some poor woman was in the way, and indignation blazed inside me. For Edwina's lover to deceive his wife was one thing, I thought heatedly, but to make her suffer was, to my mind, unforgivable. Edwina had been right to protest and I knew she would never be a willing party to the break-up of a marriage. She would never let the other woman be needlessly hurt.

I dressed slowly and as quietly as I could and when I reached the sitting-room, Edwina was perched on the arm of a chair, staring miserably into the empty fireplace. She turned suddenly as I entered and alarm showed clearly in her eyes.

"Kathy! I didn't know you were up. How long have you been awake?"

"Not long."

The nonchalance in my voice amazed me.

"But what on earth are you doing, Edwina, sitting there in your nightie?"

"I . . . the phone rang," she faltered.

"Oh? I didn't hear it."

I was surprised how easily the lie sprang to my lips.

"Who was it, Edwina?"

"I don't know. When I got downsairs they'd rung off."

"I see."

So that was the way it was going to be? She was still determined to keep me in the dark, but I let it pass, unchallenged.

"You look frozen, Edwina. Pop back into bed and I'll bring you a breakfast tray up."

"No! No, I can't do that. I have to go out."

"But I thought you didn't work on Saturdays? What about the lazy weekend we were going to have?"

"It won't take long, Kathy. I've suddenly remembered there's something that won't wait. I really must go out."

I shrugged my shoulders resignedly.

"Will you be back in time for lunch?"

"I don't know. I don't know how long I'll be. But don't

bother cooking anything for me, Kathy. I can always open a tin."

"Are you going to one of your shops?" I pressed, disliking myself intensely for what I was doing.

"Yes, the Leeds boutique."

"Right, I'll get you something to eat then, before you go."

Edwina got to her feet. Was it only imagination or was she deliberately avoiding my eyes? If only she would tell me, I fretted. Why couldn't she trust me, her oldest friend?

"Just a cup of coffee, Kathy," she said, over her shoulder. "I don't have the time for anything else and anyway, I'm not hungry."

I shrugged and turned to the empty fireplace. Small wonder, I reasoned, that Edwina's figure was slight and slim as a reed. It was easy, when she seemed never to be hungry.

I sighed, then removed the ashes from the grate and laid the fire. When finally Edwina made her appearance the logs were snapping and spitting cheerfully and the coffee was percolating on the hotplate.

She was wearing corduroy slacks and a husky sweater that seemed to accentuate her slimness and her car-coat was slung over her arm. It struck me at once that it was a mode of dress that was hardly suited to a business meeting.

She lit a cigarette and took the coffe cup I handed her with barely audible thanks.

"I'll be back as soon as I can, Kathy."

Then she picked up her coat and bag and was gone before I could think of anything to say.

I watched from the window as she backed the car from the garage and turned it expertly in the narrow lane. She was almost out of sight before I realised that the road she had taken was not the one that would take her towards Leeds.

Mystified, I flung open the front door, reaching the garden gate in time to catch a last sight of her car as it climbed the uneven winding track that led upwards to the hilltops.

I had long since realised that Edwina was never going to confide in me about her lover and I accepted it, for her private life was her own affair, uneasy though it seemed to make her. But as I walked slowly back towards the house, I felt a great sadness. Edwina had deliberately lied to me about her destination, and that I could not understand.

When Edwina returned to Keeper's a little before noon she seemed quiet, but I was glad to see that some of the tension of the early morning had left her.

She drank the bowl of soup I heated for her, then munched absently on a celery stick. For a little while she hardly spoke at all and it took a great deal of effort on my part to prevent myself from asking her, even casually, how her trip to Leeds had turned out. But I didn't ask because it would have only have invited prevarications and more awkward silences just when it seemed that wherever she had been and whoever she had met, she seemed to be much more relaxed. Her private life was her own afair, I told myself yet again, and hadn't I problems enough of my own, without taking on Edwina's?

So I watched patiently as she lit a cigarette, holding the match until the flame almost burned down to her fingers. Then with a swift, sharp puff she blew it out and threw it into the hearth.

It was such a trivial incident; done so precisely yet with such unconcern, it seemed almost that in blowing out the match, Edwina had finally reached an irrevocable decision.

She pulled deeply on her cigarette then blew out the smoke in little puffs, watching it curl upwards to the beams.

"I'll put your hair in rollers later, if you'd like," she said suddenly.

"We're still going out tonight then?"

"Of course we're still going out," she replied sharply. "Any reason why we shouldn't?"

"No, I countered, still off-balance. "No reason at all."

I bent to pile logs in the hearth, carefully avoiding her eyes, trying to gather time in which to adjust to the about-turn in her mood.

There was still so much I would have liked to ask, for I wanted so desperately to help her. If only she could bring herself to confide in me, I reasoned, maybe just to talk would have helped.

But did Edwina need my help? Had she, without any advice from me, made up her own mind? Edwina was stronger than I—she always had been. Edwina was the type of woman who went her own way, making her own mistakes and asking no one but herself to pay for them.

It was I who had been weak, running without hesitation with my problems to Michael Carter. Mike had helped me more than he could know.

A feeling of pleasure wrapped itself around me as I recalled his name, and though I knew it was wrong, it was useless to deny I was hoping, deep inside me, that he too would be one of the Saturday-night gathering at the Old House hotel. Mike, who seemed to stand for all that was safe in my troubled life—a man I had met just four short days ago yet whom I felt I had always known. I had thought when I came to Slaidbeck that Edwina would help me, but her life, it seemed, was complicated as my own. Had it not been for Mike's intervention, I might not have tried so readily to come to terms with my problems, could not have found this strange new courage that warmed and comforted me.

I shook myself mentally. I was kidding myself. If I were to

be brutally honest, I would have to admit that Mike Carter had not intervened in my life. It had been I who had thrust myself into his. He had been kind to me so I had run to him, confident that it was only his professional help I was seeking. He had given me that help as I knew he would and, try as I might, I could read no more into it than that.

Nothing had happened that was anything other than professional concern for my well-being, yet I was acting like a starry-eyed adolescent, just because this man had shown me understanding. The whole thing was ridiculous, I argued mentally. Mike Carter was an attractive man — I'd have needed to be blind and stupid not to acknowledge the fact, but in doing so, I didn't have to become infatuated. It was obvious that Mike didn't find me attractive and even if he did, I shrugged, there was one point of paramount importance I seemed bent upon ignoring. I was a married woman and for all I knew, I thought with a feeling of sick despair, Michael Carter's affections could lay elsewhere.

Suddenly I became aware that Edwina was watching me. I smiled awkwardly and rose stiffly to my feet.

"I was looking for pictures in the fire," I hazarded.

"Were you, Kathy?" Edwina asked softly. "And what did you see there?"

I shook my head.

"Nothing, Edwina. Nothing at all. Perhaps you don't get pictures with pine-logs."

"Or perhaps it only works for children and lovers?"

I felt my colour deepen and I was glad she could not see into my mind.

"You could be right," I hedged.

Then a great sadness washed over me, for there would be no pictures in the fire for me, I thought. Not now, not ever. I was married to Johnny and Johnny was alive. I had no right to think of any other man with anything other than affection, for I had no freedom of choice. I had been taught to live according to the dictates of my conscience and mine demanded that at least I should be true to myself.

Deliberately I put aside all thoughts of Michael Carter.

"What will you wear tonight?" I asked Edwina, just a little too brightly.

She stretched slowly and gracefully as a cat.

"I think," she said, "I will be dramatic tonight. I think I shall wear black."

"And I," I replied, desperately trying to match my mood to hers, "will wear my beautiful new dress."

We smiled into each other's eyes, false smiles, each of them.

I was glad I couldn't see into Edwina's heart nor she into mine.

SEVEN

The night was crisp and cold and stars sparkled frostily as
Edwina parked her car on the gravelled forecourt of the
Old House hotel. I loved the sturdy old building on sight. It
stood stone-built and solid, ringed round by trees that had
doubtless been planted by some long-ago owner who knew
the viciousness of winter winds that blew from the east. A
soft, discreetly hidden floodlight gently illuminated the
ivy-clung stones, and worn mullions and time-trodden steps
gave the hotel the welcoming air of a home.

I wondered about all the families who had lived in it and
loved in it over the years and if its last owner had been sad
when eventually it had been sold to some anonymous
consortium and added to their chain of hotels.

"It's beautiful," I breathed, strangely sad, for my heart
echoed, 'Yes, and romantic, too.'

"Thought you'd like it, Kathy. Now you see why it's one
of my favourite places. Thank heaven someone had the
good sense not to change it too much. You know, I get the
feeling, no matter how often I come here, that one night I
shall step back in time and walk right into some intimate
family gathering."

We entered the large, oak-beamed entrance hall — I
couldn't bring myself to think of it as a foyer — where the
fireglow moved lazily on flower-filled copper jugs and a
dented old warming-pan.

Did they come here often, I wondered, and were they
ever alone, Edwina and her man? Did they come openly,
not caring who knew, or were their meetings on nights such

as this one and acted out by two polite, affectionate friends?

"This way."

Edwina cut into my thoughts, nodding her head in the direction of a low, iron-snecked door.

"Cloakroom's over here. We'll leave our coats then grab a sherry while we're waiting for the others to get here."

"The others? What others?"

Mike, perhaps?

"Oh, you know. The usual crowd," Edwina shrugged. "You'll like them."

The cocktail lounge was furnished with black oak and low, chintz-covered settees and chairs. Hunting prints and old guns clustered the walls and pewter tankards hung crookedly on hooks over the bar counter.

Had people once sat cosily in the smoke-smudged ingle, sending hot pokers sizzling into jugs of ale, I mused, as they plotted for King Charles — or Cromwell — or talked of the days when hunted priests had been hidden in disguised cupboards?

"Hi, Edwina! Over here!"

Edwina guided me towards the corner where already some of her friends waited, and soon I was a part of the noisy, carefree circle. Then inexplicably I had the certain feeling that something wonderful was about to happen. My fears and worries seemed suddenly to belong to another Kathleen Parr and I found myself believing that from this moment onwards, things were going to come right for me.

Someone handed me a drink, smiling a welcome, and I found myself liking Edwina's friends immediately. There were several young married couples amongst them I noted speculatively as I sipped my sherry with near-contentment. Had one of those apparently devoted husbands phoned Keeper's Cottage only this morning? Was there, in that gathering, some woman who was unaware that her husband had driven out to meet Edwina on the lonely hill-road? Was that woman the one who talked to me excitedly of the old water-mill they were painstakingly converting into a home, or perhaps she was the fair-haired, red-cheeked farmer's wife or the dark-eyed beauty who wove cloth in her barn-studio and whose husband, I learned, was a textile designer?

But there was no way of knowing and it wasn't my business; that had been made clear enough. I was being foolish to bother with the intricacies of Edwina's love-life when I had worries enough of my own to contend with. And hadn't I decided to forget everything for just a little time and enjoy tonight to the full, even if Mike Carter wasn't there?

Carefully I studied the menu a waiter handed me, scolding myself that all that mattered at the moment was whether to order duckling or pheasant. And I wasn't stealing glances in the direction of the door because I was hoping that suddenly it would open and Mike would be standing there. Of course I wasn't! Why would I do that? I was married to Johnny, wasn't I?

We ate our meal at small, intimate tables, screened by the high backs of the cushioned settles on which we sat. Candles flickered in flower-posy holders and from somewhere near at hand came the soft sound of an orchestra. It was all so right, I thought, for those who were lucky enough to love and be loved.

Then someone ordered another bottle of wine and I didn't protest when my glass was filled again. I began to feel more and more relaxed, as though at last I was coming alive. Or maybe I could have, if there had been someone special beside me; some man whose eyes would have held mine in the candlelight, telling me mutely that I was loved. But there was no one and I tried to convince myself it was stupid to hope that Michael Carter might yet arrive. Why should he? Maybe he had some other date. Perhaps there was some other place where lights were soft and waiters hovered discreetly out of earshot. I was so sure that my hopes would come to nothing that when Mike suddenly appeared, apologising for his lateness, my heart exploded with joy. Our eyes met for a brief moment and I didn't care that my pulses were beating deliciously or that my cheeks flamed as he smiled in my direction.

I wondered if he would ask me to dance with him and a shiver of delirious happiness caused me to catch at my breath and will myself to be calm.

And when he did ask me I knew that my answering smile was a little too eager and that I rose too quickly to my feet. I didn't care that I went so readily into his arms or that the nearness of his body should not shock me into instant sedateness. I only wanted to feel close to him, be as one with him. Just for tonight, I promised silently, whilst the air shimmered with a special magic; for just this, the first and last time, I would let myself be engulfed by the madness that had taken hold of me. And so, when he drew me close to him and rested his cheek too near to mine, I offered no resistance.

I moved my head slightly.

"Hullo, Doctor," I whispered. "Glad you could make it."

Mike's hand tightened round mine, and his lips were close to my cheek as he whispered:

"Glad you're here . . ."

We didn't speak again. I closed my eyes and my body became light as a thistle seed. When the candles had burned low and the party was over, then and only then I would let myself doubt the wisdom of my actions. Right now I was in Mike's arms. The lights were soft and the music was music for lovers. Tomorrow seemed a long way away and I wanted it never to come.

We danced together for the rest of the evening, saying little, not wasting our closeness on words. None of our party seemed to notice or to care. They had paired off on the small dance floor or wandered back into the lounge.

Only Edwina seemed unaffected by the intimacy of the Old House. She sat with a young unmarried couple, their heads bent together, sketching what seemed to be dress designs on the backs of menu-cards. I thought from the safeness of Mike's arms that she looked strangely alone and vulnerable. Poor Edwina. She had most of the good things in life. She had material things in plenty yet tonight she was lonely and alone in a room crowded with laughter and happiness.

"You danced a lot with Mike Carter," she remarked as we sat by her hearth, drinking a last cup of tea together.

"Yes, he made a good partner. We danced well together," I prevaricated. "Thanks so much for a lovely evening, Edwina."

I busied myself with the teapot, trying to make my voice sound casual. I wanted, now the evening was over, to go to bed and be alone with my thoughts and perversely I wanted not to be alone so that I couldn't let myself remember Mike Carter and his nearness.

"Did Mike tell you why he was late in arriving?"

I said that he had.

"It was Dickie Hatburn—he had a toothache."

"A toothache? Mike was called out on a Saturday evening for a toothache?"

Edwina's voice was derisive and disbelieving.

"He wasn't called out. Mrs Hatburn arrived at the surgery I believe, just as Mike was leaving. Dickie was in great pain, Mike said, and the dentists were all closed up until Monday. Mike said he put a temporary dressing in it."

"I see," Edwina shrugged the matter away. "So you enjoyed the dance, Kathy?"

"Oh, yes," I breathed, willing my eyes not to shine. It had been so wonderful, but now it was over.

I lay awake for a long time with my thoughts.

"You look very beautiful," Mike had said.

Had it been the dress Edwina had chosen for me or the kindness of the candlelight? Had I really looked beautiful? Had that glow been there — the inner glow that lights the face of every woman in love?

In love?

The realisation hit me like a splash of ice-cold water. I lay stock-still for a moment, shocked that I could even have thought such a thing. I couldn't have fallen in love with Mike Carter, not in a few short days. He had helped me professionally and that was all. He was my doctor whilst I stayed in Slaidbeck. He would have done no more and no less for any other stranger.

But surely tonight had been different, the woman inside me pleaded. Mike had danced only with me. Had it been out of pity, perhaps, to help me enjoy the evening? It was the sort of thing a kind person like Mike would do, I reasoned dubiously.

But had he needed to hold me so close or brush my hair with his lips? And when our eyes met as he helped me into Edwina's car, had I only imagined that long, tender glance? But perhaps Mike treated all the women he knew that way?

I didn't know the answer and I didn't want to know, for part of me surged with happiness whilst the rest of me ached with misery. I understood now some part of the torment Edwina must feel. She loved a man she could not marry and now I was faced with the same desperate problem. Try as I might, I couldn't delude myself any

103

longer. I was in love — truly in love — with a man I scarcely knew yet one I felt I had loved since the beginning of time. I trembled at the touch of someone to whom I was no more than a name on a temporary medical card; a case of interest. I wanted Michael Carter with all my heart and I was married to Johnny Parr who did not love me.

The dim ceiling shifted and blurred in a prickling of hot tears.

"Dear Heaven," I whispered. "What am I to do?"

I awoke to a morning grey as my mood. Outside, the trees stood bare and still, their branches glistening black in the drizzling rain. The hills sat sombre, their tops wreathed in a veil of mist. Even the sparrows were still and silent. It seemed as if the whole of the countryside had caught my melancholy and was grieving with me.

I dressed with disinterest and walked quietly downstairs. Edwina had expressed a wish to sleep late and I was sorry that I had not been able to do the same. I had lain awake into the small, lonely hours of the morning, debating silently the situation in which I now found myself.

In one short week my whole world had turned upside down. I had sensed danger, felt the icy finger of fear that trailed down my spine. I had doubted my own sanity, been rebuffed by the barrier around Edwina that silently warned me to keep my distance. And in the middle of it all, safe and sane in all the doubt and fear and torment, there had been Mike. Dear kind Mike of the gentle smile and the clear, calm eyes; a man in whose arms I had felt a sweet upsurge of love and security that defied all harm. Mike, whom I must not love.

With a cluck of annoyance I filled the kettle and set it on to boil, tightening my lips and tilting my chin. Last night was over. It had been a small, sweet bonus and nothing more. I must learn from Edwina that grasping at love that is not for the taking brings only heartache.

I wandered into the sitting-room, drawing back the curtains, plumping cushions, emptying an ashtray. I felt curiously numb, as if the swift surge of ecstasy I had felt last night had flamed too fiercely and drained me of all feeling. I was glad that it was so, for in blotting out all emotion I was left with a strange detachment; a feeling that whatever was to come I could now face calmly. And I must face it alone, too. I could no longer lean on Mike for I knew that from now on I must avoid him at all costs.

The sharp rat-tat on the front door jerked me to earth. I heard the clicking of a latch-key in the lock and walked into the hall to find Mrs Hatburn standing there. I would never, I thought, get used to the countryman's habit of knocking and entering without invitation.

"You're up then?" she remarked.

I smiled. I liked Mrs Hatburn.

"Miss Howarth is still in bed. Can I do anything for you?"

"Well, it's like this."

She took off her hat and laid it on the small table, walking ahead of me into the kitchen. She did it automatically, as though that particular room was her own domain.

"My Dickie has been up half the night with a bad tooth."

"I'm very sorry," I said, inadequately.

Mrs Hatburn nodded her head wisely.

"And so is Dickie," she retorted with an air of relish. "I told him he'd be sorry but he wouldn't listen. 'Sweets aren't good for you,' I've always told him. But the young ones never take heed of good advice until it's too late."

She walked over to the cooker.

"Were you thinking of making tea, Mrs Parr? I see you've got the kettle on."

Without waiting for my answer she set two cups on the table, talking volubly as she did so.

"'Serve you right,' I said to Dickie, 'if Doctor Michael has gone out. You'll have to grin and bear it, my lad!' But the doctor was in and glad I was of it, too, Mrs Parr."

She poured milk into the cups.

"My, but he's a grand gentleman, is Doctor Michael."

I wanted to agree with her with all my heart but I could only nod my head.

"How is Dickie feeling this morning?"

"Oh, not so bad, I think, but I'll be glad to get that dratted old tooth of his seen to."

She poured the tea then reached for the biscuit tin.

"That's what I came about, Miss. Tomorrow is the day I do for Miss Howarth and I'll not be able to come until Tuesday. Got to take Dickie to the dentist in Skipton tomorrow, you see."

"Miss Howarth won't mind, Mrs Hatburn. I'm sure she'll understand why you can't come."

"Well, that's all right then."

She dipped into the biscuit tin and settled herself for a chat.

"I'll just finish off this cup, then I'll be away."

"Does Dickie like sweets, Mrs Hatburn?"

"That he does. I suppose it's on account of him not growing up properly, if you see what I mean. He's still a child in his likes and dislikes."

"But don't you think it might be better for you to give him apples instead? They'd do him more good than sweets."

"Bless your life, Miss, I don't give him sweets."

"Then what caused the toothache?"

"Well, that's it, you see. It was treacle toffee that was the

106

trouble. Been buying it every day, so I've been told from Elsie at the Post Office."

The small, plump woman nodded her head forcefully. "Bought a packet of treacle toffee every single day last week, if you like!"

"But where did he get the money?"

"You might well ask, Mrs Parr dear, and you'd get a silly answer, same as I did. I don't like Dickie telling lies—he doesn't usually tell me untruths. It's got me worried, I can tell you."

I didn't speak but waited as she stirred her tea aggressively.

"'Don't you know it's wicked to tell lies, son?' I asked him, and he said cross-his-heart, he wasn't telling lies. Said a man gave him the money!"

"A *man*?"

"That's what he said, love. This man gave Dickie the money and told him not to tell anybody about it. Said it had to be a big secret between him and Dickie."

"But why would anybody do that? I don't see the point."

"No, and no more do I. 'And who is this man?' I said, but Dickie wouldn't tell me. There's no such man if you ask me, Mrs Parr. It's my belief the lad stole the money. Where else would he get it? It's got me fair worried, I can tell you."

There was something about Mrs Hatburn's story that stirred me to curiosity. I wanted to know more. Inside me I felt a vague unease and I knew I had to get to the bottom of it all, probe the mystery of Dickie's secret.

"I don't know anyone who would have given him the money, Mrs Hatburn, but I'm a stranger to Slaidbeck," I returned dubiously. "Do you honestly think, though, that Dickie is capable of stealing?"

"No, Miss, I don't; not really. But why should he make up a story about a man that lives in the barn?"

107

"The barn? *The tithe barn?*"

I felt a shock of fear. My instinct had been right.

"That's where Dickie said the man lived. It's an unlikely story, if you ask me. There was a time when tramps and roadsters would sleep in there, but not these days. There's few tramps about, now."

"What was he like, this man in the barn?"

"There *wasn't* a man, Mrs Parr. Stands to reason, don't it?"

"All right, maybe there wasn't a man," I said impatiently. "But what did Dickie *say* he looked like?"

"Can't rightly remember. All I could get out of the lad was that it was a secret. More than that he wouldn't say. And he can be as stubborn as a pot-mule, can Dickie, when he's a mind to be."

"But can't you see, if someone is sleeping in the barn and he didn't want anyone to know he's there — well, he would bribe Dickie to keep it quiet, wouldn't he?"

Mrs Hatburn pursed her lips and placed the lid on the biscuit tin very firmly. Then she rose to her feet and collected the tea cups.

"It's no use your trying to stick up for Dickie, Miss," she retorted with a subject's-closed air. "I know he's not as bright as most, but he's got to learn the difference between right and wrong."

"But do you think Dickie is telling lies? Are you sure you haven't forgotten anything? Any little thing Dickie might have told you?"

"I don't think so."

She gave me a quizzical glance.

"You'll pardon me for saying so, Mrs Parr, but don't you think you're being just a mite too interested in the whole thing?"

I shrugged my shoulders with feigned disinterest.

"No," I lied easily. "I was only trying to be fair to Dickie, I suppose."

108

"Well, it's good of you, Miss, and I appreciate it, but I can't for the life of me imagine a man living in that draughty old barn. Not in the middle of November!"

She walked into the hall and arranged her hat, jabbing it firmly with a large hat-pin.

"See you Tuesday, then."

She opened the door, then stopped suddenly and turned round.

"I've just remembered something. That man in the barn —"

"Yes?"

"Well, according to Dickie, he was wearing a red jumper."

"A red jumper?" *A red polo-neck sweater?*

"That's what I said," she confirmed, striding towards the gate. "As if *that* makes any difference."

The cold slap of fear I expected did not come. I think I had known all along I had been right, that day Edwina and I walked down the lane.

"Oh, but it does make a difference, Mrs Hatburn," I whispered to her indignant, retreating back. "It does to me — a very great difference."

Johnny was alive and in Slaidbeck. I knew it now without the shadow of a doubt.

EIGHT

We spent a strange Sunday—Edwina subdued and with an air of sadness about her—myself almost totally preoccupied with what Mrs Hatburn had told me. Several times during that day as we lazed before the fire, I had to choke myself into silence. I wanted to talk to Edwina about the man in the red sweater. Now I could insist that he was no longer the product of my frightened mind; that a man *was* living rough in the old barn and buying Dickie Hatburn's silence. Mrs Hatburn had heard about him and she could lend substance to my story.

But I couldn't bring myself to do it, for Edwina had chosen to deny that man's existence. Could I have said:

"Edwina, there *was* a man by the barn that day. Perhaps you didn't see him, but I saw him and now Dickie has seen him, too."

But who would take any notice of Dickie who lived in a child-world of his own? Dickie Hatburn, Edwina would probably say, had been seeing things all his life. Dickie was mentally retarded and anyone who believed him was stupid.

So I shrugged inwardly and merely told her that Mrs Hatburn had said she wouldn't be able to come the following day. The news seemed to irritate Edwina out of all proportion.

"But I have to go out," she complained. "It really is too bad of her."

"But why shouldn't you go out?" I retorted. "You leave things to her when I'm not here. Why is it too bad of her?

She's got to get Dickie's tooth attended to."

"I didn't want to leave you — "

She stopped suddenly, biting off her words.

"Leave me, Edwina? But I shall be all right."

"No — I meant I didn't want you to spend the day working in the house. You see, Kathy, I must go out tomorrow. I really must."

She seemed vaguely agitated.

"But I won't be working in the house all day and of course you must go out. A business won't run itself. I wouldn't expect you to stay here with me."

"Then you're sure you'll be all right?" Edwina pressed.

"I'll be fine," I insisted. "I'll have a lovely lazy day, if that'll please you, and read through some of your magazines. Maybe I'll wash my hair . . ."

"Well, I won't be gone too long and there'll be no need for you to go down to the village, Kathy. There's loads of food in the house. You *will* be all right?" she asked yet again.

"*I'll be all right*," I asserted firmly, and that should have been the end of the matter. At least it might have been if I hadn't had the feeling that Mrs Hatburn's absence the following day wasn't at all to Edwina's liking and that for some reason she didn't want me to go to the village.

Sunday grizzled into Monday, chill and damp and cheerless. I sat on the window-seat and watched as Edwina's car disappeared into the thick mist.

I sighed, strangely satisfied. Now, with Edwina gone, I was free to do something on my own, for I had to find the man in the red sweater. How I was to do it I had no idea, but find him I must. I had to know once and for all time, whether or not it was Johnny.

I shook my head. I *knew* it was Johnny. What I had to find out was exactly what game Johnny was playing.

The telephone, that perverse invention that only came to life on Edwina's departure, decided for me. Its sudden ringing shocked me out of my uncertainty.

Of course, it could be Mike. Oh, it must be Mike! I wanted so much to hear his voice. The resolve that I must not think of him was forgotten. It was easy to have decided to put him from my mind; not so easy when suddenly he was there, at the other end of the line.

Joyfully, I snatched up the receiver then waited impatiently for the pips to end. Mike? Ringing from a call-box?

"Hullo?" I whispered. "Kathleen Parr . . ."

There was a silence, then the magnified sound of long-indrawn breath. I waited, the animal fear crawling beneath my skin again. Then it came, shrill and distorted but unmistakable.

I'll take you home again, Kathleen . . .

I closed my eyes, willing myself to be calm as the whistling echoed inside my head, holding tightly to the chair as my knees buckled beneath me. My lips were stiff, my mouth suddenly dry. Cupping my hand over the mouthpiece, I drew a long, steadying breath.

The ticking of the mantel-clock filled the room and my heart thumped in crazy rhythm with it.

A voice whispered, "Kathleen?" then nothing, save the click of a replaced receiver and the purring of a dead line.

For a moment, fear clutched at my throat and paralysed every part of my body.

"No!" I gasped. "Oh, no!"

Trembling, I lowered myself into a chair, still clutching the receiver in a hand that shook uncontrollably.

"Johnny!" I almost sobbed.

There was no doubting that one whispered word, no mistaking the warning message. Johnny was close at hand and he had whistled as he always did when those dark eyes narrowed dangerously and the blackness possessed him. He must be so near that he had seen Edwina leave.

He had made the call from a public phone. Frantically I tried to remember having seen one. There must be one in Slaidbeck but I didn't know where.

I wiped the moist palms of my hands down my skirt and desperately tried to calm the panic that choked in my throat. I had resolved so bravely to search for the man who slept in the barn, to do my utmost to bring the matter into the open. Now Johnny had issued a challenge and it was suddenly a different matter. My bravado was gone and the whole of my body churned with fear again. For one small moment it was my impulse to ring Mike, but I realised almost at once that I had no right to involve him so deeply in my affairs — affairs that promised danger. I was on my own, now. It was my problem and I would have no peace of mind until I had settled it my own way.

Almost without realising I was doing it, I collected the breakfast dishes on to a tray and carried them into the kitchen. Automatically squirting soap-liquid into the sink, I turned on the taps. The simple task of washing cups and saucers and plates gave me an oblique kind of detachment and helped me to arrange the turmoil of my thoughts into some kind of order.

Johnny was not in Iran. He was here, in Slaidbeck, and just a few moments ago he had telephoned me. Somehow, he had found me and for almost a week had chosen to play a cat-and-mouse game. What was in his mind, I couldn't even begin to guess at for there seemed to be no explanation for his actions. All I knew with certainty was that whatever his plans were, he had made them with care. To fake his own disappearance, leaving a trail of misleading evidence behind him and to contrive to arrive in Slaidbeck at almost the same time as myself had been no chance of circumstance.

What Johnny was about, I couldn't understand, nor, I thought, dare I even begin to try. I only knew that outside, in the grey misty day, a man was waiting for me. That man was my husband. Briefly we had loved and I had borne his son. Surely that must count for something? Whatever Johnny intended to do, I could not think he would hurt me. Johnny could fight with words, could fashion derision and contempt into vicious darts that could wound as surely as the most painful of blows. They left no scar or bruise and there was no defence against them. I knew this only too well, but I could not bring myself to believe he would harm me physically.

What then was I to do? Just a few minutes ago, I had been ready to go in search of Johnny. Now I was not so sure. I had lulled myself into a feeling of false security—for a little while even, I had found a modicum of courage. But Johnny hadn't changed. Johnny still knew how to strike stark fear into my heart.

I reached for a cigarette and lit it with fingers that were still unsteady. I pulled hard on it, drawing the smoke into my lungs, and felt a giddiness in my head. I thought of the wise old saying, 'When in doubt, do nothing.'

Should I then do nothing? Should I stay here, safe from harm inside Keeper's Cottage until Edwina returned?

A harsh banging on the front door echoed through the house and brought a stifled gasp of fear to my throat.

Not Johnny? *Oh, please, not Johnny?*

Quickly I turned the key in the back door and slid home the bolt. Edwina had slammed the front door behind her. It was almost certain I was safe.

Gently I walked into the hall, my eyes on the flap of the letter-box. It wasn't the postman. The postman had been. It couldn't be Johnny. It *mustn't* be Johnny!

Slowly and carefully I walked up the stairs, then, reaching the turn at the half-landing, I flew to the safety of

Edwina's bedroom. With fingers stiff with fear I opened the window.

"Who is it? What do you want?"

"Mrs Parr?" called a voice, a blessedly strange voice. "Mrs Kathleen Parr?"

Carefully I leaned over the sill and looked down. The man on the doorstep was dressed in a plain grey suit and carried a briefcase. By the garden gate I could just make out the dim outline of a strange car.

"Who are you?" I insisted, my mouth still dry.

"If you would give me a few minutes of your time, Mrs Parr — just a few details about your husband . . .?"

Then he smiled up at me.

"Oh, I should have said," he added apologetically. "I'm from Eastern Oil."

He reached down into his pocket and held up a card and once again the tenseness left me, leaving me weak, like a deflated balloon.

"Just a minute," I gasped, the relief in my voice obvious. I shut the window and hurried downstairs.

"Sorry," I lied glibly. "I was upstairs, making the beds."

If my excuse sounded a little thin, I didn't care. It was all right. It wasn't Johnny, just someone from Johnny's employers. Maybe now I could talk to this man, tell him what I knew, pass on the burden and the worry to him. But the old animal instinct urged caution.

The man followed me into the sitting-room and sat down in the chair I indicated.

"I wasn't expecting anyone from Eastern Oil," I began, my voice light with relief. "I've already told them all I can."

I had to be careful. I had thought about telling the truth about Johnny; it would have been the most sensible and honest thing to do. But would this man believe my story? Could I convince him about the man in the barn, the whistling, the one whispered word, *Kathleen?* Wouldn't it all have sounded too incredible? Wouldn't they have doubted my reason, dismissed it as the hysterical rantings of an unbalanced woman? I knew somehow that I must not risk it, that for the time being, until I had positive proof, Eastern Oil would have to work things out for themselves.

"Yes, Mrs Parr, but could you tell it again to me? Something that at the time slipped your mind — something you missed?"

He was looking directly at me in a defiant, almost challenging way.

I said:

"Look, I really don't understand the reason for this. I've told your Welfare Department everything."

Suddenly I felt a flash of suspicion. My fear was gone. I think I had reached the point where I no longer cared — the point of no return, perhaps. I knew now it must all come out into the open so I had nothing to lose, had I, by trying?

"But surely," I hazarded, trying to keep my face a blank, "you know all about it? Didn't Mr — er — I forget the name of the man who came. He was tall, very tall, with thick red hair. Mr Davies wasn't it, from your Welfare Department?"

The man nodded.

"Yes, I read Davies' report, but I think perhaps if you told me?"

But I wasn't wholly listening, because the kind and elderly man from Eastern Oil's Welfare Department had been white-haired and slight and his name was not Davies, but Jackson.

Calmly now, so that I could hardly believe it was myself who was speaking, I said:

"Now please tell me who you *really* are and who sent you? You're not from Eastern Oil, I know it!"

He sprang to his feet then and stood looking down at

me. I tried to match his gaze but I had to tilt my head awkwardly to do it and it seemed to give him the advantage.

Slowly I rose to my feet then deliberately lifting my chin I looked him full in the face and said:

"I shall call the police."

I picked up the phone but he placed his hand across the cradle and blocked the line.

"Don't do that, Mrs Parr," he said softly. "I have no quarrel with you. I just want you to give a message to your husband."

"My husband is missing. He's in Iran—they don't know where he is . . ."

"So you're in it too, are you? I'd have thought he'd have kept it quiet from you."

"What do you mean?" I demanded. "Kept what quiet? I know nothing about it, I tell you. *Nothing!*"

For a moment he looked at me, then, mimicking my voice, he said:

"I know you're there, Johnny. I've heard you and seen you by the barn."

He paused to smile slowly.

"I know you're not missing and I know about the money."

The phone call! my mind shrieked. Friday night, just before Edwina got home! I'd thought it was Johnny, then decided it had been Edwina's lover. Edwina had been agitated—I'd been so sure.

"*You?*" I whispered incredulously. "*It was you?*"

He nodded.

"Me, Mrs Parr, so don't bother denying anything. Now, shall we start all over again. The money? Where is it?"

"Look—I'm not sure about anything," I hedged, playing for precious seconds in which to think. "I heard a man whistling—whistling a tune that made me think it was

117

Johnny, and I saw a man by the old barn that *could* have
been him."

"You know it was him."

"No I don't — not for sure," I gasped. "Edwina didn't hear
the whistling and she said there was no one by the barn."

"Johnny's around, Mrs Parr. You know it and now I know
it, so where's that money? You told me about it-
remember?"

"You mean the money in Johnny's bank?"

In spite of everything my heart gave a little skip of
triumph. If I could keep this man from finding out that
the money was in my name, I thought . . .

"Lady, I don't know where he's got it. I only know that
there should be close on fifteen-thousand pounds and half
of it's mine!"

I nodded agreement.

"Yes, that's right. There's fourteen thousand pounds in
an account in Johnny's name — I found out by accident. I
didn't think he had so much money. I certainly didn't
know some of it was yours."

"Half of it, Mrs Parr. *Half* — "

I was chancing my luck but I was winning, I knew it. For
once in my life I was holding my own and I was sure I had
managed to convince the man that the money was beyond
my reach.

"All right," I said quickly, "half of it's yours. But will
you tell me one thing, please? Where did you get it? That
kind of money doesn't grow on trees. The bank manager
wasn't very happy about it either. I went to see him about
it when I found the statement in Johnny's desk."

"Johnny's a fool," the man spat out bitterly. "There was
no need for it to be put into an account. A safe-deposit box
would have been better."

"Oh, yes," I challenged. "Best not to leave any records
about when it's hot money."

For the first time he showed anger. Grabbing my wrist he pulled me close to him, thrusting his face into mine.

"Yes, it's hot money, so don't you ever forget it or maybe you'll find yourself an accessory!"

A streak of answering temper made me fling my wrist downwards, freeing it of his grasp.

"Accessory to what?" I demanded. "Tell me what Johnny has done. I want to know. *I really want to know!*"

The man shrugged, calm again. I picked up Edwina's cigarette box and offered it to him. Elated, I saw my hand was steady as I held it.

He took a cigarette and fumbled in his pocket for matches. Then he sat down in the chair again and looked up at me.

He was older than Johnny, I realised for the first time. About forty, I'd have said. And he had the same sun-tanned face. He too worked abroad.

"Yes," he returned quietly. "It fits. You wouldn't know, would you? You'd be the last to be told, in the circumstances."

I demanded that he explain himself.

"What are you trying to imply? What circumstances?"

"Look — I worked with Johnny. I knew how things were between you. Sometimes when Johnny had had a few too many drinks —"

"Johnny didn't drink. Not all that much, anyway."

I tilted my head again, saddened that I knew so little about the man I had married. But I didn't propose to discuss our sordid quarrels with a stranger.

"We were talking about money," I cut in ruthlessly. "And I don't know your name, either. I like to know who I'm talking to. It helps, you know."

"McIlroy," he returned, briefly.

I nodded, satisfied. It matched the slight Irish lilt.

"How did you get the money, Mr McIlroy?" I demanded.

119

"At least I have a right to know that. Other people might ask me. I'd have to know what to say."

"Other people? What other people?"

His head jerked up and his eyes narrowed speculatively.

"I don't know, yet. But you've got this money dishonestly and who's to know who else may be looking for it?"

"*Has* anybody been asking questions?" he snapped.

I looked him straight in the eyes.

"No, but they might."

He believed me, I was sure of it. I felt I wanted to burst with triumph. For the first time in my life I was winning! I was right on top!

"All right, Mrs Parr. I reckon you're on the level. I don't think you knew what Johnny was up to."

"Johnny and you," I corrected.

"All right then. Johnny and me. We did a job for someone—a favour, you might call it."

"Nothing violent?"

I remembered Johnny's moods and felt a prickling of alarm.

"Nothing violent, Mrs Parr. Just a little game, shall we say, between me and Johnny on the one hand and Her Majesty's Customs and Excise on the other."

"You've been smuggling?"

"That's about it. Not what you'd call a crime, the way most folks look at it. We've all of us done it at some time or other, haven't we?"

I remembered the large bottle of expensive perfume bought on our honeymoon weekend in Paris. I'd gone through the 'Nothing-to-declare' gate all wide-eyed and innocent. Oh, yes, we had all done it at some time or another. But more than a bottle of perfume was involved this time, there was no getting away from it.

"What did you get through Customs that earned you fourteen thousand pounds?"

I begged his question.

"Fifteen thousand, Mrs Parr, only we had expenses, shall we say?"

McIlroy smiled as if they had done something clever. He's as crazy as Johnny, I thought wildly. I took in a deep breath then stood unspeaking, waiting for the answer to my question.

McIlroy smiled again.

"Does it matter?"

"Yes, it does. It matters very much to me. Was it drugs?"

"Oh, no, not drugs. They're too hot on that . . ."

"Then *what*?"

I was being stupid—utterly stupid. The more I knew the more precarious my own position would become. An accessory, hadn't McIlroy said? But I had to know.

He looked at me for a moment, then, shrugging slightly, said:

"Gold bullion. Quite a lot of it. Oh, and a hundred thousand pounds in emeralds. Hot emeralds."

"All stolen?" I whispered.

"No. Just the emeralds." He smiled as if he'd said something humorous. "And we didn't nick 'em. Johnny and me just brought them through Customs."

He said it without remorse and suddenly I wanted to get him out of the house. I said:

"Look, I don't want to hear any more. I don't know where Johnny is except that I'm almost sure he's around here somewhere. Your chances of finding him, Mr McIlroy, are better than mine, I'd say. But if he should get in touch with me, what will I tell him?"

"Just tell him Mac wants to see him. Tell him I'm staying at the Swan in the village and to leave a message for me there. Better still, tell him I'm sleeping at the back, over the small lounge, if he's interested. If he's as fond of whistling as you say, Mrs Parr, tell him to whistle me a little tune when he sees my light go on, eh?"

He rose to his feet and smiled. It was a deceptively gentle smile that told me in no uncertain terms exactly where I stood.

"And you'll be careful, won't you, my dear? Don't get over-inquisitive or anything and you'll be all right."

He tapped his nose with his finger and smiled again.

"Just tell Johnny I called. Don't mention it to anyone else, eh?"

"If Johnny contacts me, I'll give him your message," I hedged. "But tell me one thing, Mr McIlroy? What made you come here looking for Johnny? How did you know where to look?"

He turned on the doorstep and looked down into my eyes with nothing short of amused contempt.

"You mean you don't know? You *really* don't know? Oh, my God, you silly little bitch!"

Then he laughed softly and was gone. I heard the clicking of the garden gate, then the revving of his car engine. I couldn't see him properly for the mist had thickened and everything was indistinct and colourless. It made me think I was looking at ghosts. I even began to think I had imagined it all, that McIlroy had been a ghost, too.

I slammed the front door quickly. I *had* dreamed it, I thought wildly. My imagination was working overtime again. I was mad, no matter what Mike said.

Cigarette smoke hung in small drifts in the sitting-room when I returned, and in the ashtray a cigarette end still smouldered. I hadn't imagined anything. I wasn't mad. I was a silly little bitch . . .

I gave an exclamation of annoyance. This time I had had enough. I was safe for the moment but only until

McIlroy found Johnny and learned that I had the money. I'd have the two of them on my back then and that I couldn't handle. I had to find Johnny before McIlroy found him. For the time being the money was my insurance and Johnny wouldn't harm me as long as I had that. I'd find him. I'd promise him anything. I'd tell him about McIlroy; tell him I would draw out the money and meet him in London with it. I'd promise my silence and beg him to get out of my life for ever. Then what would I do? Go to the police? Tell Eastern Oil? I honestly didn't know. But I'd got to find Johnny.

I was afraid again, but I'd put on my coat and close the door firmly behind me. I would walk down the garden path and out of the gate and I would—what would I do, then? What would I do when I stood alone in the vast outside, when the safe walls of Keeper's Cottage no longer encircled me or the thick oak door no longer stood between me and danger? What would I really say to Johnny if I found him and what would Johnny say to me?

Being brave, I told myself, wasn't going to be easy, not when I had to face Johnny. I could, if I wanted, think up a dozen different reasons why I should stay here safe inside this sturdy little house. I could find countless excuses to keep me busily occupied within sight and sound of the telephone until Edwina returned. I could, if I were stupid enough, pretend that none of it had happened. I could convince myself that Johnny had not spoken my name this morning or that the man who called himself McIlroy had never sat by Edwina's fireside or smoked one of her cigarettes.

But I was deluding myself and I was wasting time. I remembered what McIlroy had called me and it stung me into action.

So I threw on my coat and slipped the spare front-door key into my pocket, then quickly, whilst my meagre

123

courage lasted, I walked towards the door. For just a moment I hesitated, then, squaring my shoulders in a gesture of defiance, I slipped the latch and closed the door quietly behind me. I was alone in the silent, fog-shrouded day and there could be no going back, now.

NINE

My feet rustled a drift of wet, fallen leaves and the damp
air was cool on my burning cheeks. I pulled up the collar
of my coat and dug my hands into my pockets. I had left
my gloves behind me but I knew I could not trust myself to
return for them. Once inside Keeper's again, I should
never find the courage ever to leave it.

Without further thought, I walked down the garden
path and turned towards the rough, winding track that led
upwards to the moors and hills.

Away from the shelter of the house I felt a slight breeze.
It was, I realised, blowing the mists that had hung over
everything since yesterday into rolling swirls through which
I could occasionally see the outlines of trees and walls and
hilltops that not so long ago had been completely hidden.
My footsteps sounded less muffled and the feeling of
isolation that was an inseparable part of every foggy day
seemed to lift a little. Now it would be easier for me to find
Johnny.

I wondered as I walked why I had not gone first in the
direction of the barn. Surely that would have been the
most likely place in which to start my search? Was it
instinct that sent me upwards towards the open stretch of
moorland? Was it a sense of self-preservation that had
urged my footsteps in the opposite direction or was it that
McIlroy might be waiting at the barn?

I stopped short, straining to catch the slightest sound,
steeling myself to prevent that furtive glance behind me. I
would not look back, for to do so would betray my anxiety
to anyone who may be following me.

A feeling of fear rose in my throat and I fought down the urge to run, to turn and flee to Keeper's benign protection before it was too late. But a rare stubborn streak caused me to go on. There was no sound of following footsteps, only the soft, sad cry of a curlew and the far-away bleat of a sheep.

What kind of foolish game was I playing, I asked myself almost angrily! How could I be so stupid, so utterly devoid of common sense? Surely the most normal thing to do would have been to telephone London and let Eastern Oil deal with it? They had a right to know, after all, that he was here in Slaidbeck. I could tell them he had been briefly in touch with me and it would be out of my hands, then. That would have been the sanest thing to do, I urged; to go back to Keeper's and pick up the phone. It was a pity, I thought as I started the long climb towards the hilltops, that sanity and all sense of reason seemed to have completely deserted me.

I would walk on for just a little longer, I decided, to the clump of wind-bent trees that hung over the ravine. I could see ahead of me now to where the stony track that served as a road petered out and merged into the moor. I would walk that far and no farther. Then I would turn and run like the wind, down and down until I was safely home again.

At first I thought the shrill whistle I heard was that of a shepherd calling to his dog. I stopped, glad that another soul was near me, holding my breath, almost, that I might hear him.

"Kathleen! Up here, Kathleen!"

The voice came to me distinctly. It floated clearly from a distance and seemed to echo above, below and all around me. It wasn't the voice of a shepherd.

For a moment I was too shocked with fear to move. I

half turned and looked below me. I should have realised, I thought with a sob, that the wind had dropped again. I should have known that when it did, the fog would return.

No more than three minutes ago I had been able to see Keeper's behind me and Slaidbeck nestling in the hollow beyond it. Now it was blotted out, wreathed in a mist that seemed to swirl and roll towards me even as I watched. I could blunder downwards again into the fog. I could risk losing the path and wander aimlessly on to the moors. I might even stumble towards the marsh.

Mike's words rang in my ears.

Tracks through the marsh that only sheep and shepherds know. Mists that come down without warning.

I could turn back or I could go on. I had a choice between the devil and the deep blue sea.

I chose to go on and up to where Johnny waited for me. Where he waited, I couldn't be certain. I only knew he was within hailing distance, that he had almost certainly followed and overtaken me and I hadn't known it.

I looked around, wondering which would be my best way of escape, but it seemed futile to hope I might yet make a run for it. The mists had completely closed in again, blotting out everything around me. I remembered that the clump of trees had been about five hundred yards above and ahead of me. Was Johnny waiting by those trees? Should I go on or stand still? Dare I wait until he made some movement, came near enough for me to hear him, to call to him about McIlroy. The fog had cut off my escape but it was also my friend, for although I could not see Johnny, I knew it was not possible, either, for Johnny to see me. If I froze into immobility, would he betray his presence and give me some slight chance of knowing where he waited?

I was desperately afraid now. I had been foolish to try to seek out Johnny. I knew he wouldn't listen to reason for no normal man would act as he was acting now. McIlroy or not, I wasn't equipped to deal with the strange workings of Johnny's mind. I was out of my depth. I should have phoned Eastern Oil, or even the police.

Straining to catch the slightest sound, hardly daring to breathe, I started forward. My footsteps sounded loudly in my ears and a dislodged stone slipped and slithered down the track, bouncing noisily as it did so. I froze again, waiting for the movement that did not come. Carefully I sidestepped the path and felt the springy turf of the moor soft beneath my feet. Now I could walk without sound and still keep the track in sight. I felt a faint shock of surprise that I had not thought of it before. I realised I need not walk on to where I imagined Johnny to be waiting. I could turn round and, sheltered by the swirling mists, could slowly and silently follow the track down the hillside again. But something inside me warned me against it. Some strange and perverse instinct urged me not to turn my back on danger but to keep on, no matter what might lay ahead of me.

My heart beat a little less quickly now and my ears had become attuned to the awful stillness. Cautiously, with every step I took as stealthy as the movements of a wild cat, I moved forward.

"Kathleen! Up here!"

The caller was closer now. We were playing a crazy game of cat-and-mouse and I was walking into a nightmare of my own making. I had chosen to test my courage, to prove to myself I was no longer afraid; to prove to Johnny that his power over me had ended and I had failed dismally. My body shook with fear now and my clenched teeth could not hold back the cry of terror that forced itself from my throat.

"Johnny! I've got to talk to you!"

"Here, Kathleen. Over here."

128

Johnny's voice betrayed an uplift of confidence.

I was sobbing now with fear and frustration. I stumbled blindly on, drawn against my will to the disembodied voice that summoned me from the mists.

The clump of trees loomed suddenly ahead and I stopped short, my breath coming in noisy rasps.

"So you've come at last, Kathleen?"

I heard a laugh, low and tirumphant. It jolted me out of my hysteria as surely as if it had been a slap to my face, for the laughing was that of a madman. I flung my body round in the direction from which I had come. There was a slithering at my feet as the earth beneath me seemed to disintegrate. I screamed wildly, my arms clutching the air about me. I felt my body weightless for a split second before it struck the earth with a dull and awful thud.

Small yellow darts stabbed at my eyes before pain enveloped me in a dark blanket. I lay still on the wet earth, waves of red light shifting around me. From somewhere above I heard Johnny laugh again and I knew I had fallen to the foot of the ravine. I had done what Johnny intended I should do. He had lured me to the cliff-like edge and I had fallen. There would be no sign of a struggle when they found me, I thought through the haze of my pain. There had been no need for Johnny to lay a finger on me or involve himself physically in any way. I had done his work for him. He could disappear now into the enshrouding fog as stealthily and silently as he had come, and after they found my lifeless body and when the time was right, he could come back from his self-imposed oblivion and claim the money he had placed in my name.

But I wasn't dead! How far I had fallen, how badly I was hurt, I couldn't tell, for I seemed incapable of movement and my whole body throbbed with an agony of pain that was almost unbearable. *But I was not dead.*

Faintly again through my pain, I heard the soft almost

indulgent laugh and willed myself into silence. Then Johnny started to whistle, each note clear and deliberate, a song of triumph.

I'll take you home again, Kathleen . . .

I listened as it faded slowly away into the mists. Mike had told me about the uncaring hills and the treacherous fogs that could catch a stranger unawares. But those mists had protected me and now they shielded me from sight. If I lay quite still, if I fought the overwhelming desire to surrender to pain and darkness, those mists might yet be my salvation.

How long I lay there not daring to move, I had no way of knowing. When finally I felt again the fresh wind that blew in my face, the sky was visible again and darkening into late afternoon. There was no sound but my own rasping breathing and I could see I was quite alone. Cautiously I moved my arms and legs, carefully I bent my elbows and levered my aching body into a sitting position. In the fading light I could see the edge of the ravine and the stunted trees above me. I had fallen from a great height yet it appeared I had only bruised and jarred my body into merciful unconsciousness. I felt the hard ground on which I lay with disbelief. My body throbbed with pain and cold yet by some miracle I was still alive.

Johnny had gone. He had not tried to find me or to help me, I realised with growing horror. He had left me lying there, not caring if I were dead or alive. I had thought he would never harm me but I had been wrong. Johnny had merely been waiting for the right moment. He had seen me leave Edwina's house and knew the time was right. I wondered what might have happened to me if the fog had not come down again, and I knew that had Johnny and I come face to face I would have had little chance of survival. I would always be grateful to that eerie, swirling mist.

Now, if I could find my way back to the track again, if Johnny did not return to gloat over his triumph, I might yet reach safety. In my pocket lay the key to Keeper's sturdy door. It felt cold in my hand and my fingers tightened around it and clutched it as though it were a talisman.

Slowly I limped in the direction of the track. I looked at my watch and found to my joy that it had not been broken by my fall. The fingers pointed to three-thirty. Edwina might be home now, might even be alarmed by my absence. I prayed with all my heart she would come in search of me, for my body hurt unbearably and tears of pain and fear flowed down my cheeks. I knew that if I ever reached safety again there would be no choice but for me to take strong and serious action. For Johnny's sake I must do this, for clearly he was in need of help. Nor for my own safety could I ignore the money. The police would have to be told. Johnny must be restrained and helped before it was too late.

A sharp pain tore at my back again and I fought it with all the strngth I could summon, for I dare not let myself weaken.

When eventually I saw the lights of a car cutting through the gloom I had barely strength left to stay on my feet. I heard the sharp squeal of brakes and the opening of a car door. Dimly I saw Edwina's white face swim before me. There was the sound of urgent running footsteps then strong arms caught and held me, and as the blackness enveloped me I imagined I heard Mike's voice:

"Kathy, darling. Thank God you're safe!"

I think I shall never again see so welcoming a sight as the dear walls of Keeper's Cottage or feel so safe as when the old oak door slammed behind us, shutting out all that was fearful and evil.

"What in heaven's name possessed you to go out alone?
What on earth were you doing on the hills on a day like
this?"

Edwina's voice was sharp with anxiety.

"Anything could have happened to you!"

I nodded mutely, fighting back the tears of blessed relief
that sprung readily to my eyes. Edwina could not know
how nearly right she was!

Gently Mike helped me out of my coat.

"It's all right, Edwina. She's safe now and that's all that
matters."

He took a long look at my torn and mud-stained
clothing. I had not noticed it before, but my tights were
ripped and bloody from an ugly gash on my leg.

"Lie flat on the floor, Kathy, and we'll see if there's any
serious damage."

Expertly Mike's fingers probed and kneaded my body,
pausing as I winced with pain as he gently manipulated
each joint. Eventually he said:

"Well, there's no broken bones but you'll be a mass of
bruises in the morning. What happened to your leg. How
did you fall?"

"I went over the top of the ravine, near where the track
ends. I fell to the bottom."

"The ravine? You fell over the top? Kathy, you could
have killed yourself!" Edwina gasped. "Are you out of your
mind?"

I shook my head slowly.

"No," I said softly. "Not any more."

Mike helped me to a chair and took the brandy Edwina
had poured, gently holding it to my lips.

"You can drink this now," he said, "and then I think a
cup of very sweet tea would fit the bill very nicely."

He smiled into my eyes and the love I felt for him spilled
out of me uncaring. I leaned my head on the back of the

chair and closed my eyes. Funny, I thought, but not so very long ago I had imagined I heard a voice, rough with concern, saying '*Kathy, darling* . . .'

But the world had been swimming about me then and Edwina's face was a white blur that shifted before my eyes. My mind had played a trick as I slipped into unconsciousness again, of that I was now certain. I hoped, with a feeling of unease, that I hadn't said anything stupid in return. But Mike hadn't spoken those words. They had been born of my longing and the hopelessness of my love.

"Heavens, I'm a mess," I said, looking at myself properly for the first time. "My clothes are ruined. They'll never come clean again!"

"Clothes are easily replaced," Mike retorted. "Right now, I think you should have a good hot bath. It'll help to ease your bruises and clean that gash on your leg. And put plenty of antiseptic into the water."

Edwina poured out tea. She had been strangely quiet and her hands shook as she passed the cup to me. I wondered how soon it would be before she demanded I should tell her the truth about what happened, why I'd really gone out in the fog. I needed time to think and I didn't want to talk in front of Mike, either. But there were questions I must ask, eventually, and I hoped that Edwina could help me to find some of the answers.

"I'll have to go now," Mike said. "Monday evening surgery is usually a full one but I'll be back as soon as I can, Kathy, to dress your leg. Dry it gently and cover it meantime with gauze. I'll bring an anti-tetanus injection with me, just to be on the safe side."

He picked up his coat.

"See she gets into bed and keeps warm," he said to Edwina. Then he gave me a brief smile and was gone.

"Thanks, Mike. Thanks a lot," I called, but already he and Edwina were walking down the garden path, and by the light from the window, I could see them talking earnestly together.

I felt better for the long hot bath but I refused to go to bed as Mike had ordered.

"No, Edwina," I insisted. "I don't care what Mike said. I'm feeling better now — just a bit stiff, that's all."

I struggled into a pair of slacks and pulled a sweater over my head.

"This cut isn't too bad now and, besides, I want to talk to you."

"Talk to *me?*"

I heard the unmistakable indrawing of Edwina's breath.

"Well, talk *at* you, I suppose. I want you to listen to me. I've got to get things straight in my mind. Just listen, if you will, and shoot me down if you think I get too badly off course."

"I don't know what you mean, Kathy," Edwina's voice was anxious.

"I'm not sure that I do either. But something is very wrong and I've got to work it out, somehow. Today for instance — "

"Yes?"

I didn't reply, but concentrated on hopping clumsily down the stairs, hanging on to the banister-rail as I did so. My leg hurt more than I cared to admit.

"What about today?" Edwina insisted when we had settled ourselves comfortably. "Just what happened up there on the moor, Kathy? You've no idea how I felt when I got back and found you'd gone. Thank heaven for Mike! I'd never have found you if it hadn't been for him."

I took a long, deep breath.

"I'm grateful to you, Edwina, but I've got to get one thing straight, right from the start. There have been times during the last week when I have doubted my own sanity.

134

It was as bad as that. But I know, now, that I was wrong. Today, when I went out . . ." There was a loud knocking on the door. Simultaneously, our heads jerked upwards.

"Mike?" I asked. "So soon?"

Edwina rose to her feet. "I'll let him in," she said. I thought she seemed relieved by the interruption.

I shook my head, wearily. I had been determined to talk the whole thing out; even to tell Edwina about McIlroy. I needed her advice now, for something had to be done quickly. Now, glad as I was to see Mike again, it would have to wait a little longer, for I wouldn't, I resolved, involve Mike.

The long silence caused me suddenly to turn my head. In one crazy, fear-filled second I saw Edwina's white and anxious face, crumpled into a picture of utter defeat, and by her side, from the doorway, a man looked down at me.

His eyes were narrowed viciously and the smile that quirked down the corners of his mouth was nothing new to me in its mocking indolence. He was unshaven and unkempt. He was wearing a red sweater.

"Hullo, Kathleen," the voice drawled.

I struggled to my feet, closing my eyes against a wave of terror that washed over me, setting my heart thumping afresh and my ears ringing with a warning of fear.

I clung to the back of the chair, steadying myself, willing myself to sleak his name.

My lips moved despairingly.

"Johnny?" was all I could say.

TEN

Suddenly the room was filled with the familiar smell of danger. I read fear in Edwina's face and with sickening despair I knew that I couldn't rely on her support. Already, it seemed, she had sensed the tension that heralded the onset of one of Johnny's moods and stood there taut and silent, her eyes shifting warily between Johnny and me.

My body grew limp. I felt I had been drained of feeling; as though all resistance was gone and nothing was left inside me to care any more. I became aware that I had been more upset than I would admit by the events of the day. My head throbbed intolerably and my brusied body ached with a dull, insistent pain.

"Well, Kathleen?"

Johnny's words were softly spoken but they cracked like a whiplash in my stupefied brain.

Looking into the dark eyes above me, I heard myself whisper:

"What do you want, Johnny? Why are you doing this?"

He shrugged his shoulders and a fleeting gleam of amusement showed in his eyes. He was enjoying, as he always had, the upset he was causing. I ran my tongue round my lips, then said:

"Edwina—this is Johnny, my husband."

It seemed incredible to me that at such a time I should be making a formal introduction as though we were at a party. I wanted to laugh hysterically as Edwina silently inclined her head and Johnny acknowledged her presence with a lifting of his eyebrows. Then Edwina dropped her eyes to the floor as if passively refusing to take any part in what was to come. I was truly alone, but at least I felt that Johnny wouldn't try to harm me now. However impartial Edwina intended to remain, her presence would at least ensure my safety, I felt.

"Why haven't you been in touch with Eastern Oil, Johnny?" I demanded, forcing myself to speak slowly. "Don't you think they should be told you aren't missing any longer?"

I was surprised by the calmness in my voice. I wondered if it deceived Johnny.

"My dear Kathleen, I wasn't aware I *was* missing. I merely decided not to go to Abu Dhabi, that's all."

"So you could fix your disappearance elsewhere! *Why*, Johnny? What made you do such a thing? How *could* you?"

The indolence of his reply had stung me into action. It gave me a brief flash of courage.

"Have you stopped to think how much trouble and worry you've caused?"

"Oh dear. Were you worried for me?"

"No Johnny. Never. Not for a moment!"

"Now there's wifely concern for you."

A small mocking smile briefly moved his lips.

"Really, Kathleen, you're a great disappointment to me."

"Am I? Why is that? Is it because I'm here now instead of lying at the bottom of the ravine?"

Edwina gave a small, choking cry. I had almost forgotten she was in the room.

"Kathy! Johnny!"

Her hands fluttered in agitation.

"Why don't we all calm down? Why don't we have a drink?"

She looked at me with mute appeal in her eyes. It

137

shocked me that she could go to pieces so completely.

"Yes please, Edwina," I replied briefly, shocked to realise that I really wanted one.

I saw that her hands were shaking as she passed me a brandy then poured out whisky for herself and Johnny. For a moment no one spoke. I gulped at my drink and it burned my throat.

I had to know what was in Johnny's mind. I had to find some way to jolt him into the open, wipe the false, bland expression from his face.

"Why did you try to kill me today?"

I hurled the question without warning and saw a slight tensing of his nostrils, sensed a momentary slipping of his guard. Then the mocking smile was back on his lips again and he answered easily:

"Kill you, Kathleen? Why should I want to do that?"

He shook his head with exaggerated surprise, then said gently: "You're not still imagining things, are you? You'll really have to learn to control yourself or one day I'm going to lose patience with you."

I didn't explode with indignation as I thought I would.

My new sense of self-preservation warned me that I should tread carefully. The tingling in my spine was back again and it forced me to speak firmly and clearly.

"I don't know why you should want me dead, Johnny, and I don't care much about your non-existent patience because this afternoon I wasn't imagining anything. You knew I was on the edge of the ravine—you intended it that way. You manoeuvred me there very cleverly and if I hadn't lost my footing you'd have . . ."

"Oh, Kathleen—*please*—"

He spread his hands in a gesture of bewilderment, then gazed appealingly at Edwina, his face a mask of martyrdom.

See what a wife I've got? his eyes demanded. *What am I to do about her?*

"Did you think you could get away with it, Johnny? This afternoon, on the hilltop, did you honestly think you'd succeeded? Hadn't you the sense to realise that I wouldn't have come looking for you without good reason? I wanted to warn you, though why I should have I don't know. You're in trouble up to your neck and I should have left you to stew in it!"

Now all pretence was gone. The show that was being staged for Edwina's benefit was over. I'd cornered Johnny and his face whitened into anger, his eyes narrow with contempt. I shuddered involuntarily, for the hatred in them was terrifying in its unguarded intensity.

"So? The kitten has claws? You're almost human, Kathleen when you stop cringing!"

I felt a shiver of anxiety. My mind was a crazy turmoil of fear and anger and apprehension. I took a long, steadying gulp of air.

"Don't you realise what you are doing? What do you think will happen when the truth comes out?"

"I don't give a damn!" Johnny snarled. "I'm sick of lickspittling to bosses. I'm sick of being sent to some sweating hell-hole to drill for oil or drill for water!"

There was anger in his voice now, white-hot and vicious. Every instinct in me urged caution. I was shaking inside with stark terror yet I knew I dare not show the least sign of capitulation.

"What do you want, Johnny? Do you really think life owes you something?"

"Yes, it does, and I'm going to have it! For a start, I want some money, Kathleen!"

"Fourteen thousand pounds, perhaps? The money you made sure I'd find? How did you get it? Tell me," I demanded. "Go on—*tell me!*"

I stood tense, waiting for the torrent of hatred to break, but it didn't. There was a moment of stillness, then Johnny spoke and his voice was quiet again and soft and dangerous.

"I won it. I won it at roulette — a bit of luck, you might say."

Briefly I closed my eyes. I couldn't believe the ease with which he could lie. Either he was utterly without conscience or he was sick.

"I don't believe you, Johnny. Tell me where you really got it!"

I didn't imagine the flicker of alarm that showed in his eyes. It was brief and guarded but I saw it and it gave me a crazy surge of triumph.

"Tell me about the game you played with Customs," I pressed. "Tell me about the emeralds — a hundred thousand pounds in emeralds. Johnny! Tell me about McIlroy!"

"McIlroy?"

The word came in a hiss of anger. It seemed to echo round the room then spiral towards the ceiling like a sharp-tongued dart. I waited, wide-eyed and unmoving as Johnny slowly walked towards the chair by which I stood. He fixed me with a slanting stare and I was powerless to move. Then suddenly his hand grasped my wrist. I cried out with mingled pain and terror. Johnny's face was so close to mine that I could feel his angry breath on my cheek.

"What about McIlroy?"

Brandy spilled down my slacks as the glass went spinning from my grasp to shatter on the hearthstones. I cried out with pain but the vice-hard grip did not relax for a second.

"I said, *What about McIlroy?*"

I screamed, "Let me go . . ." then fell backwards as Edwina darted forward and shook Johnny's arm so that he suddenly released me. The impact sent a fresh wave of pain through my aching body as it hit the chair again and I shrank back, pressing myself into cushions, trying to stifle the sobs that were tied in a hard, painful knot in my throat.

"Stop it, both of you!" Edwina pleaded, her voice harsh with fear, but Johnny shook off her hand and stood over my chair, looking down at me with a hatred that was beyond belief.

"Where's McIlroy? What did he tell you?"

"He told me about the money," I whispered, "and how you got it. And he wants his share, Johnny. He's at the Swan—the pub by the church. You're to get in touch with him there, he said."

"He'll get no money!"

"He meant it, Johnny. He said half of it was his. You'd better see him—tell him you'll meet him in London and give it to him there. It'll give you a chance to get away . . ."

"And you?" he flung at me. "What'll you do?"

I clutched tightly at the arm of the chair. I think I shall never be so brave again. Quietly I said:

"I shall go to the police and tell them what I know. I won't give you or McIlroy a penny of that money, Johnny. It isn't mine to give."

"No—it's mine!"

"It isn't, Johnny. It's dishonest money and I'll not be responsible for handing it over to you. You put it in *my* name in *my* bank and that's where it will stay until the police tell me what to do with it!"

My mouth was dry again and I couldn't say another word. I had no need to, for Johnny's hand caught me in a blow that sent pain stabbing through my head. I bit on my lip with terror but I refused to let myself cry out. For a mad, nightmare moment I thought he would strike me again, then Edwina's scream pierced the near-oblivion against which I was struggling.

"Johnny! Oh please, *please* stop! I won't listen! I can't take any more! You must go; go at once!"

She wrenched open her handbag and pulled out an envelope.

"Here—take it! It's all there. It should see you over—"

She thrust the packet into Johnny's hands.

"Take it, but *go*! You can have the car."

She flung a bunch of keys to the floor.

"Get the night train and leave the car at the station. Do anything, but *go* . . ."

"Edwina," I gasped. "What are you doing?"

But she didn't hear me. She was looking at Johnny and for a moment she held his eyes with her own, the agony in them was unmistakable.

"Please go?" she whispered.

I watched bemused as Johnny placed the envelope in his pocket and stooped to pick up the keys from the floor at Edwina's feet without protest.

Then he turned to me and I saw the look of evil that twisted his face. It was so awful that my blood ran cold.

Thus quietly and without another backward glance he left the house. I heard the slam of the car door and the wild revving of the car. I could neither speak nor move. My body seemed not to belong to me any more and I sat unmoving as Edwina sagged into a chair and buried her face in her hands. Then she raised her eyes to mine.

"He couldn't have stayed, Kathy. It wouldn't have been right. He had to go."

"Yes," I said numbly. "It wouldn't have been right. But why did you do it, Edwina? Why did you give him money? It *was* money, wasn't it? And your car—why did you let him take that?"

Edwina dropped her eyes again, twisting the ring on her finger, shrugging off my question.

"Kathy," she said, hesitantly. "Today, on the moors—I

142

want you to tell me what really happened. I must know. It's important."

I wasn't able to reply for the banshee screaming of brakes froze us into a startled alertness. There was a split second of silence as we stood, tense and listening, then the sickening, tearing sound of shattering metal.

Edwina jerked to her feet, her eyes wide with fear, her face a mask of horror.

"No!" she whispered. "Dear God, no!"

She flung her body across the room. I could hear the shuddering of her breathing as she stood, still as a statue in the open doorway, listening. Then the roar of an explosion was followed by a flash of light. From beyond the garden wall came the reflection of leaping flames and I smelled the unmistakable smell of burning petrol. Edwina gave a sob of despair.

"Johnny!" she screamed as she lunged forward. "Johnny?"

I will never forget that crackling, all-devouring fire or the pathetic silhouette of the inert body that slumped over the wheel for a brief moment before it was engulfed by the inferno around it. I shall remember too that it was Edwina and not I who tried to reach Johnny before the searing heat drove her back.

"Do something!" she screamed wildly. *"For God's sake do something!"*

Then the paralysis that had rooted me to the spot released its hold and I dragged Edwina away from the blazing car.

"Stay there!" I gasped as I ran back to the telephone. "Don't go any nearer!"

Like an automaton I watched fascinated as my finger dialled for help. The calm, impersonal voice that answered my call took over completely, sorting out my incoherent gasps, asking for the number of my telephone and the location of the accident. It took several seconds for me to realise that an ambulance and the fire brigade were already being alerted. I stood numb, the room about me taking upon itself an alien strangeness. This, I thought wildly, is a waking nightmare. It isn't happening. But the dull glow that illuminated each tiny window-pane jerked me back to reality and I felt the uneven cobbles of the garden path beneath my feet as I ran back to where Edwina stood, her arms limp by her sides, staring into the blaze. I couldn't speak and reached for her hand, holding it tightly in my own. Together we stood as the flames licked upwards to the sky.

Far below us, beyond the village, I watched fascinated as a blue flashing light threaded steadily nearer, heard the wail of a siren, saw blazing headlights.

A car-door slammed then someone was running towards us, and through a mist of blessed relief I saw Mike's face.

"Was that the ambulance I heard?" he asked. "Did you phone them?"

I nodded, swallowing hard, my throat dry with terror.

"Yes, they're coming, and the fire brigade. How did you know, Mike? Did they phone you, too?"

"I didn't know, Kathy. I was on my way to see to you."

He jerked his head in the direction of the blaze. The flames were less intense now and a black cloud of choking smoke blew towards us.

"That's Edwina's car. Which of you was driving? Is anybody still in there? Is anybody hurt?"

Edwina didn't move or speak. It seemed she hadn't heard Mike or even noticed his arrival.

"Johnny's in there," I choked. "My husband. Edwina gave him the car. We couldn't get to him — it was too hot — we couldn't get near . . ."

"Your husband?" Mike gasped, then shaking his head he said softly:

"Poor devil."

Then turning to Edwina, he grasped her arm and shook it.

"Go back to the house, both of you," he ordered abruptly. "I'll see to things here."

I placed my arms round Edwina's shoulders and guided her up the lane and through the gate.

Someone was standing in the shadows, but I was so weary now, so immune to further shocks that I wasn't afraid as he stepped into the light that streamed from the open doorway.

"Dickie! What are you doing here?"

He didn't reply but followed us like a small, frightened puppy into the house, standing there, awkwardly twisting his cap in his large, ungainly hands.

I drew the curtains across the window, shutting out the nightmare and closed the door on the turmoil that had now invaded the quiet of the lane.

"Go home, Dickie," I said as I seated Edwina by the fire. "You can't stay here. Go back to your mother."

But he stood his ground, his round, open face distorted with misery.

"It wasn't my fault," he stammered. "I didn't do it on purpose."

"Didn't do what, Dickie?" I asked. "What do you mean?"

"That man, Miss—the man that lives in the barn. He took Miss Howarth's car. I saw him getting into it and I tried to stop him. But I didn't make him crash into the wall!"

I knew then what it was all about. Dickie had been outside when Johnny left. He must have thought Johnny was stealing the car and tried to stop him driving away. Had Johnny skidded and crashed, trying to avoid Dickie? It was all too much for me to take in. The happenings of the

145

awful day seemed suddenly to overwhelm me. If I let myself, I thought wildly, I shall scream and scream until I am hoarse. I shall run out of this house and go on and on until I drop. I shall find some place to hide; some place that is far away from Slaidbeck and Johnny and the awful carnage out there in the lane.

But something of the new creature inside me took hold of my reason and willed me the strength to go on for just a little longer.

"It's all right, Dickie," I whispered. "It's all right. Just go home now, there's a good boy.

I took him by the arm and led him to the back door.

"It isn't nice in the lane, Dickie. Go out this way and over the fields. No one will be cross with you, I promise."

He stood for a moment.

"I came to tell you about the bird," he hesitated. "It's better now. I let it go and it flew away . . ."

"Yes, Dickie, but can you tell me about it another time?" I said, tonelessly. "Just go home now, there's a good boy."

He left then, without another word.

I lifted the kettle and filled it at the tap.

Tea, I thought. Strong, sweet tea. That's what you need for shock, isn't it?

Edwina was still staring into the fire when I carried in the tray.

"Drink this," I said, softly, wrapping her fingers round the mug and guiding it to her lips. "It's not too hot," I urged. "It will do you good, Edwina."

She gave me a small, sad smile.

"Thanks," she whispered. "Is there a cigarette about?"

I reached for the box, then snapped the lighter, helping her trembling hands as best I could.

Somehow I forced myself not to think; to do the things I would have expected Edwina to have done. I carried a jug of tea to the firemen who stood now by the charred skeleton that had once been Edwina's car and watched as the inert form wrapped round in grey blankets was lifted into the waiting ambulance. My body throbbed with the pain of my fall and my mind seemed not to be my own. It was as if the Kathleen Parr I knew was standing aside from it all, protected inside a bubble of anonymity, and the other woman — the one who lived inside her — had taken over completely. It was that inner woman who kept her head, made tea, stood quietly by Michael Carter's side, now. She didn't want to be sick at the horror of it all or wonder how much more the awful day could bring.

Mike laid an arm on my shoulders.

"It was over very quickly, Kathy. Nothing you or Edwina could have done would have helped him."

I nodded, glad of his comfort.

"He didn't suffer?"

"No, Kathy. I think he was unconscious, at the very least, even before the fire started."

We walked towards the house. Mike said:

"I'll come in for just a minute, then I'll follow the ambulance to the hospital. I'll do what's necessary there, Kathy. It'll be better that way."

"Thank you," I whispered. "I don't know what I'd have done if you hadn't come when you did."

"It'll be all right."

He gave my shoulder a reassuring squeeze.

Edwina looked up as we entered.

"He's dead, isn't he?"

It was more a statement than a question.

"Johnny's dead?"

Mike nodded.

Edwina rose to her feet, straightening her back, almost visibly willing herself into mobility.

"What happened, Mike?"

"I think the car skidded. There was probably mud on

147

the road. The police are doing what they can. They'll find out."

I remembered what Dickie Hatburn had told me about that skid, but nothing could be gained, I thought, by involving him. Tomorrow, if I had to, would be time enough to tell them about it. Tonight, I seemed incapable of any further explanations.

"Would you like a drink, Mike?"

Already Edwina had uncorked a bottle and poured a generous measure for herself.

"No thanks. But how about putting the kettle on whilst I have a look at Kathy's leg. That's what I really came for, come to think of it."

Edwina did as Mike asked. She seemed now to be coming out of the shock that had completely paralysed her in the lane.

"The car's a write-off, I suppose," she said flatly from the kitchen.

"Afraid so."

Mike was dressing my leg now.

"It seems clean, Kathy, but I'll give you that injection, just to be sure."

I nodded, unspeaking. I didn't want to move again. I wanted to sit with the softness of the chair cocooning my sore and aching body. I wanted to sleep there by the fire because I didn't know how I would find the strength to climb the stairs and take off my clothes.

"What must I do now, Mike?"

I had not experienced death so close to me before. I didn't know where to begin or even what to do. I only knew that this was something I couldn't run away from.

Mike smiled reassuringly into my eyes.

"Nothing at all except go to bed and try to sleep. I'll do what's to be done tonight. Tomorrow, you'll be better able to face things. I'll tell you about it then."

I nodded.

"Is Edwina all right?" I asked. "She was very upset, when it happened."

"I'll give you both something to calm you down and help you to sleep. Right now, if you'll just see the police sergeant and give him some particulars, it's all you can do tonight. I'll be up in the morning as soon as I can, Kathy."

"Thank you, Mike, and bless you," I whispered.

It seemed there was nothing more to say.

ELEVEN

I lay awake into the small morning hours. The tablet Mike gave me had blunted my senses but still I couldn't sleep. I stared at the dim ceiling, wondering why my mind was so numb, my body so far away from my thoughts. I wanted to straighten out the muddle that spun round and round in my head, think of all that had happened that day and its dreadful consequences, but I could not. Try as I might, I was unable to arrange the turmoil inside me into any kind of order.

There was so much I didn't understand, so many little doubts that niggled below the surface. What had happened to Edwina? Why, these last few days, had that facade of brittle efficiency crumbled to show the uncertain person she had become? Why had she given money to Johnny? Johnny, my husband who was dead.

But it wasn't my husband they had wrapped round in blankets and taken away. It was *her* husband — the husband of the woman who lived inside me; the woman who said things I dare not say and thought things I dare not think. I was glad it was her husband because then I didn't have to cry for Johnny. Kathleen Parr could remain apart and numb and unbelieving.

I shook my head with impatience, then willed my body to be still. I wanted to toss and turn and thump my pillows in anger and dismay but every movement was now an agony of pain.

Could it only have been a few short hours ago, I thought with disbelief, that I had blundered in the fog towards that

150

tantalising voice? Was it only this morning — no, yesterday morning — that I had been suspended so briefly between life and death as my body hurtled to the bottom of the ravine? By what miracle was I still alive?

If I lie quite still, I wondered, if I listen hard enough, will I hear it again, that whistle in the dark?

But Johnny was dead and the woman inside me must mourn for him. I, Kathleen Parr, lying dry-eyed in the night, could not acknowledge his passing or show pain or grief. Nor would I ever know the reasons for his behaviour or find the answer to all that had happened during the past week.

Could it only be one week since I had fled to Edwina and Keeper's Cottage? I hoped to find refuge in Slaidbeck but I had rushed headlong into a danger far worse than I could have imagined. I had feared for my life, yet it had been Johnny whom capricious Fate had beckoned.

I gave a small sigh of annoyance. I was becoming maudlin. I was, in some strange way, willing myself to accept the burden of guilt for Johnny's death. The tablet Mike had given me was causing it, I was sure. I wanted a drink — a hot drink would make me feel better.

Snapping on the bedside light, I eased my stiff, cold body into my dressing-gown, hugging it to me for comfort. There was nothing to be gained by lying brooding in the darkness.

I walked as quietly as I could to the head of the stairs, but Edwina was not asleep. A shaft of light shone from her half-open door.

"Is that you, Kathy? Are you awake, too?"

I pushed her door further open, nodding silently.

"I'm going downstairs to heat some milk. Shall I do a glass for you?"

"Please."

Edwina sat up in bed, arranging her pillows behind her.

"Will you bring it up? Can you manage all right? We could talk for a while, if you'd like that?"

I wanted very much to talk and I wanted Edwina to talk to me.

"Yes," I said, "I'll be fine."

I settled myself in the chair by Edwina's bed and tucked her eiderdown round my knees.

"I feel more comfortable sitting here," I remarked.

"Are you in much pain?" Edwina was at once sympathetic.

"Nothing I can't put up with, I suppose. And when I think what might have happened . . ." I shrugged. "Well, what are a few bruises and cuts?"

Edwina looked thoughtful for a moment, then said:

"Tonight, Kathy, just before—"

She stopped and I could see she was fighting for control of her emotions.

"Before the car crashed?" I prompted gently.

"Yes," she whispered. "Well, I was just going to ask you what happened when you got lost on the moors, why you went out there, in the first place. I'd still like to know."

I didn't want to talk about it. Somehow, it wasn't important any more for me to convince Edwina of the danger I had been in, Nothing could be gained now by talking about it.

"Does it really matter, Edwina?"

"To me it does. Please believe me, I've got a very good reason for wanting to know."

"All right," I shrugged. "This morning, just after you left the house, Johnny phoned. He just whistled—you know, the way I told you he always whistled that tune—and then he said my name. That was all."

I looked up to meet Edwina's eyes. They were kind and a little sad and now there was no disbelief in them.

"Go on?" she asked.

I leaned my head back and closed my eyes for a moment. Just to try to talk about it brought back the horror again. I took a deep breath and willed myself to go on. I told her, as calmly as I could, of my determination to seek Johnny out; of my terror when I heard his voice calling me and the awful realisation that I was trapped by the fog.

"So you see, I had to go on, Edwina. I knew it was useless to try to get away. I could have wandered on to the marsh," I shrugged. "I wasn't left with much of a choice, really. That's when I fell over the edge of the ravine. Then I heard Johnny whistling again, and laughing. That was when I knew for certain he was sick."

Edwina's face was deathly pale, now.

"And after that, Kathy? What happened then?"

"I don't know. I passed out, I suppose. There's only one thing I'm sure about, Edwina. Johnny didn't look for me or try to help me. He laughed and he left me there."

Edwina dropped her eyes.

"I'm so sorry, Kathy; so very sorry about it all. You do believe me, don't you?"

"Yes," I nodded, "and I'm sorry, too. About your car I mean, and all the trouble I've brought with me. And if you hadn't found me when you did, Edwina, I don't know what would have happened. I couldn't have gone on much longer.

Edwina studied her fingers.

"I knew something was wrong when I got back to Keeper's. I didn't know what to do, so I phoned Mike. He came with me to look for you."

"Did Mike think I was in some kind of trouble?"

"Yes he did, and so did I. You see—" she hesitated a little, then:

"I knew you were in danger because I knew you'd be with Johnny."

"You *knew*, Edwina?"

The old feeling was back again. I didn't want to know but still I asked:

"How could you know?"

"Because Johnny should have been with me, not you. I arranged to meet him in Skipton. I waited for more than an hour and he didn't turn up. I knew then I had to get back to Slaidbeck quickly and I had to crawl. I cursed the fog all the way back."

Something inside me did a somersault. I didn't want Edwina to go on. Quite suddenly, I wanted to forget the whole thing.

But for all that, I whispered:

"Yes, Edwina?"

"Johnny needed money. He was in trouble. I don't know just what it was, but I think he'd got mixed up with smuggling something in from the Middle East. He wanted to disappear for a while — someone was threatening him.

McIlroy, my mind supplied.

"How could you know about all this, Edwina?" I demanded. "*I* didn't know."

"Nor did I, Kathy, until last Saturday. Johnny told me then.

"You met Johnny on Saturday morning?"

Something suddenly clicked in my brain. That had been the day we promised ourselves a lazy day by the fireside. The telephone had rung, very early in the morning, Edwina said it was a wrong number and afterwards she had rushed out. To Leeds, she had said, but she had taken the hilltop road.

Even now something was missing; something that didn't quite add up. Whilst my instinct warned me not to ask the question, I heard my voice saying:

"Edwina. On Saturday morning you had a phone call. I asked you about it and you said it had been a wrong number."

"Yes," Edwina answered softly. Her eyes were guarded, warning me and pleading with me not to go on.

I tried to collect my thoughts. I had to be sure of saying the right thing. I had been very casual about that telephone call, I remembered. Tactfully, I had tried not to let Edwina know I'd heard part of it, What exactly had she said?

"I'll not let you hurt her! I won't have her hurt!"

I had thought the conversation had been about the other woman, the wife who was in the way. But it had been myself Edwina had defended. Johnny must have threatened to hurt me and Edwina had agreed to meet him and to give him money.

I felt a wave of love and gratitude. Dear, foolish Edwina. She had offered Johnny money so he would go away. Then a cold shock hit me and dragged me back to reality, for I remembered something else. Those words I had heard as I turned to go, quietly as I could, back to my room.

'Of course I love you. Please believe me, I do, but I didn't think it would turn out like this.'

The words sang in my ears. I shook my head. It was all too much of a muddle and I didn't want to know any more. Even so, my voice was calm as I asked.

"Funny, you know, but I heard part of what you said. I pretended I hadn't because I thought —"

I hesitated, reluctant to go on. But the woman inside me was speaking now and I couldn't stop her.

"—well, I didn't want to embarrass you, Edwina. You see, at the time, I was sure you were talking to your lover."

Edwina's eyes met mine. They were calm now and there was a look in them almost of glad resignation.

"Then you were right, Kathy," she said, quietly.

"But Edwina, I don't understand."

My body felt numb and I had to force myself to speak. "When you went out that Saturday morning, I thought

155

you were going to meet *him* — the man you are in love with."

"Yes, Kathy," Edwina whispered wistfully, her lips trembling, "that's right. I *was* going to meet my lover. I was going to meet Johnny!"

People say that time can stand still. For me that early winter's morning, I think it did. For just a little while it seemed that I was inside a great void and the world was a kaleidoscope of people living out some tragedy in which I could take no part, no interest. Then gradually I became aware of the mug clutched in my wooden hands, of the bedroom, so still that it appeared to me as a stage-set, waiting for the actors to move and speak and bring it to life. I saw Edwina's pale face and eyes that begged for understanding and forgiveness. I felt my lips, stiff with shock, trying to mouth the words I wanted not to say.

"Johnny?" I managed to whisper, at last. *"You and Johnny?"*

Edwina nodded. I waited for her to speak but she didn't. I said:

"No, Edwina! It just isn't possible! It isn't true!" But her eyes told me it was.

"How long?" I asked. "Why didn't I know! Why didn't I guess?"

But of course I wouldn't know. When your best friend and your husband —

I shut down my thoughts abruptly, then said:

"Please tell me?"

"I'm sorry, Kathy." Edwina's words were barely a whisper. "I didn't want it to happen."

I shook my head, wearily. "But it *did* happen, Edwina, and all the time, I didn't know."

I flung aside the eiderdown that covered my knees and pulled myself unsteadily to my feet. I wanted to run from that room, from the sight of Edwina's grief-twisted face, from reality itself. I stood for a time at the window. Nothing had changed. The waning moon lit the hills and trees with a strange, dim glow. Faintly in the distance, the tower of the church stabbed bluntly into the night sky.

Suddenly I wanted to laugh hysterically. None of this, I told myself, was real. I was sleeping and dreaming and soon I would awaken and hear again that whistle in the dark.

But the half-empty mug of milk was still clutched in my shaking hands and the soft carpet felt real beneath my bare feet. I moistened my dry lips and swallowed hard.

"We've got to talk," I said. "I'm not going to throw a fit of rage or scratch your face, or anything. Somehow, it was never quite real between Johnny and me. Perhaps in some way it was all my fault. But please, at least tell me about it?"

Edwina nodded and threw aside her bedclothes.

"We can't talk here," she said abruptly, reaching for her dressing-gown.

I followed her downstairs and into the warm room. In the hearth the fire still glowed faintly. Glad of something to do, I stirred the embers and piled on kindling and logs.

"When did it start?" I asked dully, staring fixedly into the small, darting flames.

"Before you and Johnny were married, Kathy. If you remember, you wrote, giving me your new address. I think you'd just gone to live at Johnny's flat. Anyway, I was in London on business and I thought I'd surprise you. You were out when I called and Johnny said you'd be gone for some time. I stayed to talk to him and we had a couple of drinks before I left. I suppose it started then."

"I didn't know you'd been," I said. "Johnny didn't tell me."

"No, I gathered that. I didn't mention it to you, either,

in any of my later letters. I think even then I realised what was happening between Johnny and me. I knew I had to cut and run before it was too late."

I understand so well, I wanted to say. I remembered that first time Johnny and I had met. I recalled his vibrant personality, his good looks and the way he made me feel beautiful and interesting—as if I were the only woman at that noisy, crowded party.

"But for all that, you still met each other, Edwina?"

"Yes. About a couple of weeks later, when I was in London again, I ran into Johnny accidentally in Oxford Street. It seemed as if we just had to meet again. He told me then that you were having a baby and that you'd both decided to get married. He was going back to the Middle East, he said, in a few days. We saw each other every day before he went."

"Yet still he married me," I whispered. "What happened after that, Edwina?"

"Oh, we kept in touch by letter and we spent all the time together we could manage whenever he got a spell of leave. I began to get the idea your marriage wasn't working out. Then, when I heard about the baby—"

She stopped and I saw that her eyes were bright with tears.

"—when I heard you'd lost the baby, Kathy, it seemed there might be a chance for Johnny and me."

"What do you mean, Edwina? I don't understand."

"By that time Johnny and I were lovers."

She made a small, helpless gesture.

"Oh, it was wrong, I know, but I think I always knew that I would never be able to marry Johnny and it seemed so little to ask. I wouldn't have broken up your marriage, Kathy. For the sake of the child, I wouldn't have done that."

"But the baby died," I said, simply.

Edwina nodded slowly.

"That was when Johnny said he wanted a divorce. He wanted then to marry me."

"I didn't know," I said flatly. "He never talked to me about it. I only knew things weren't right between us. I thought, you see, that Johnny felt trapped by our marriage. I was right, wasn't I?"

Edwina nodded. "And it was my fault," she admitted.

I shook my head vigorously.

"No, Edwina. It was nobody's fault. It just had to happen, that's all."

"You don't blame me?"

"No," I sighed. "I don't blame you, Edwina."

How could I? I knew only too well the magic Johnny could weave. He had been a perfect lover but a reluctant husband. Johnny's kind lived in a world of their own imagining and when they were faced with the stark reality of life — real life — they couldn't accept it.

Slowly, things were becoming clearer. Now I was beginning to understand. But there was one more thing I had to know.

"Last week, Edwina, when you telephoned me in London, did you know that Johnny was missing?"

Edwina raised her head and looked clearly into my eyes.

"No, Kathy, I swear I didn't. I phoned you because —" she hesitated. "I think I phoned because my conscience was nagging me. I wanted to talk to you, to find out if what Johnny said was true."

"You mean, you wanted to know if our marriage really was on the rocks?"

"Yes, that's about it. I think even then I wanted to tell you about Johnny and me. I'm not wholly bad, Kathy."

"So when I told you that Johnny was missing . . .?"

"I think I flew into a panic. I had to know what was going on. I thought that if I asked you up to stay with me,

159

at least I'd be in the picture. You see, Kathy, I was the other woman and I had no rights. I couldn't worry about Johnny—not openly, anyway. I couldn't telephone his firm and ask for news of him. Can't you see how it was with me?"

"Yes," I said slowly, "I think I can."

"Well, that's why I asked you to come to me. It seemed we needed each other."

"And you'd swear you had no part in Johnny's plan to fake his disappearance? You knew nothing about that, or the smuggling?"

I knew at once from her face that she had not.

"I'll swear I didn't, Kathy."

Her words gave me a grain of comfort but I hadn't finished. There was more to come.

"Then why, when I heard the whistling and saw Johnny standing near the barn, did you deny it all? Why did you make me think I was going out of my mind, Edwina? Had you truly no part in it?"

"Not intentionally. It must seem that way to you, now. It was my own fault, really. I did hear that whistling, but I only had your word for it that it was Johnny. I didn't know at that time that Johnny was in Slaidbeck or that you were in any danger. I'd never seen Johnny in one of his worse moods, had I? That's why I said you were imagining it."

"And the barn?"

She reached for a cigarette, lighting it carefully, watching the smoke rise slowly and disappear. Then she said:

"I shouldn't have done that. I saw Johnny as clearly as you did and I realised at once that something was wrong. I didn't know what was in his mind or what he planned. I just knew I had to play along with him, to wait until he got in touch with me and explained things. At least, I thought, he's safe—not missing or anything."

In a flash it all fitted. Johnny had come to Edwina to hide out. McIlroy had known where to find him—everybody, it seemed, had known about Edwina and Johnny except me. McIlroy's words rang in my ears.

'You mean you don't know? . . . You silly little bitch . . .!'

Fool! my mind screamed. *Blind, stupid fool!*

I stared into the crackling logs, my cheeks burning and a sick feeling rising in my throat.

"So you played for time, Edwina? You denied seeing Johnny and hoped for the best?"

"I had to. I reckoned that Johnny knew what he was doing and why he was doing it. I had to trust him."

"At the risk of my sanity?"

Edwina looked at me helplessly.

"I've said I'm sorry. We can all be wise with hindsight."

She was right and I didn't try to deny it. I was beginning to understand what had caused the tension in Edwina that had seemed so foreign to her nature. She loved Johnny as I had once done and like me she was suffering. Anyone who loved Johnny paid for it.

I buried my face in my hands.

"Dear heaven," I whispered. "What a mess. What an awful mess."

In an instant Edwina was on her knees beside my chair.

"Kathy love, what can I do? What can I say to make you believe I wouldn't have hurt you? If I told you I'd ended it all between Johnny and me, would you believe me?"

Slowly, I raised my head.

"Did you, Edwina? When did you do that?"

"Last Saturday morning. I met Johnny along the hilltop road. I knew something was wrong. I think if I'm to be truthful, that I was becoming aware of a strangeness in him. When he phoned me he threatened to harm you. At first, you see, I thought he was talking about divorce when he said you were in the way. I asked him to meet me and talk about it. I was beginning to be afraid."

"Yes, I understand, Edwina. I know about that, only too well."

Edwina stared into the fire, her body taut.

"Johnny said he was in a fix and needed my help. I couldn't make out why. He'd got into trouble with the Customs, he said. Something had gone wrong and he wanted money so that he could hide out. I said I'd get some for him when the banks opened again on Monday."

She made a helpless, appealing gesture with her hands.

"That was why he pretended to go missing, I suppose —"

"Faked his own disappearance," I shrugged, "then took the next plane back to England so he could engineer mine! How did he know I would come to you, Edwina? How could he have known?"

"He didn't know, Kathy. When he got back to England he came straight to me, then found you had arrived in Slaidbeck ahead of him. That's what he told me anyway. I didn't see any reason to disbelieve him."

I thought with cold detachment how unwittingly I had played into Johnny's hands.

"I promised Johnny money if he would go away and not harm you, Kathy. I drew five hundred pounds from the bank."

"Five hundred pounds!"

So Edwina had really thought Johnny intended to harm me?

"Oh, Edwina, so much money! You must have known . . ."

"Yes, Kathy, by that time I did. I didn't believe him, I'm afraid when he talked about all the money he'd soon be able to come by."

"The fourteen thousand pounds — oh, that was real enough," I supplied, dully. "Money for bringing stolen emeralds into the country—the money the man McIlroy wanted a share in."

Edwina shook her head.

"I didn't realise, Kathy. I just told Johnny it had to end between him and me. I said we mustn't meet again. I honestly thought if I did that you and he might get together again. I hadn't realised things were so bad between you. I suppose the money I gave him was the pay-off, as they say."

I believed Edwina. I remembered the air of utter dejection about her when she had returned to Keeper's later that Saturday.

"So you arranged to meet Johnny later when you'd got the money?"

Edwina nodded mutely.

"Was that why you were so upset when Mrs Hatburn said she couldn't come on her usual Monday?"

"Yes, Kathy. I'd figured you'd be all right if someone was in the house with you. You see, I had an awful feeling that Johnny wouldn't meet me in Skipton as we'd arranged. But he needed money so I had to go there to get it for him. I was right, wasn't I? He wanted me well away from Slaidbeck so he could get to you and I fell for it."

"And I did just what Johnny hoped I would do. I went out looking for him—me and McIlroy both, I shouldn't wonder."

I held out my hand and Edwina grasped it in hers. For a long time we sat, silent. I wondered why I had not realised the truth, why I had never even suspected that Edwina's lover had been Johnny. I understood how utterly miserable she must be feeling for she, too, had known the giddy heights and abysmal depths of loving Johnny. Now she must feel as I had felt, must know the utter despair of dead love.

"It will pass, Edwina," I tried to comfort. "The feeling of betrayal will pass. Things will start to come right, now."

I felt Edwina's hand tighten in mine, then she turned to look at me.

"But it isn't over, Kathy. I think I always knew what Johnny was like, but he was my kind of man. We were right for each other, he and I. I knew him, in the end, in all his moods, and I still loved him. I shall always love him."

Her face crumpled and her lips trembled. "It won't be over for me, not ever."

"Oh, Edwina," I whispered.

I placed my arm around her trembling shoulders and held her close. I could almost feel the turmoil of grief and guilt inside her as she struggled to control her feelings. Then she wept and her body shook with agonised sobs. I laid my cheek on her head and for me, too, came the comfort of tears. I cried then for the Johnny I had loved and for a love that had died. I cried the long-denied tears for the child we had made with that love then destroyed with our hatred. I wept as I had never thought possible because I knew that my grief was in part Edwina's grief. She had loved Johnny truly. Edwina, more than I, had the right to mourn him.

It was a little after eight in the morning with daybreak reluctantly spreading from behind the hilltops when Mike called.

Edwina had returned to her bed and I heard her gentle sobbing for a time as I sat, stunned and disbelieving still, in the big, soft armchair. For the remainder of the night I stayed by the ingle, reluctant to move other than to place a log from time to time on the fire. My body throbbed with pain and my heart ached for the mess that Edwina and Johnny and I had made of our lives. I wanted to stay inside Keeper's with the world shut out. I wanted to sit out my sorrow beside the warmth of the fireside. I wanted never

164

to have to move, to laugh, to cry or to speak again. My brain would take no more. I had suspended myself in emotional limbo where nothing mattered and nothing hurtful could reach me ever again.

But Mike's gentle knocking on the front door broke into the safety of my dream-world. With a mixture of reluctance and relief I opened the door to him and in doing so I knew I was letting in all the cares and heartache that the new day would bring with it.

"Thought I'd look in before surgery," he smiled.

Taking my hand in his, he felt for my pulse in a matter-of-fact way. If he noticed my pallor or the dark rings beneath my eyes, he made no comment.

"Where's Edwina?" he asked.

"She's sleeping, now. She was very upset but I think she'll be all right," I replied, briefly.

I didn't want to tell Mike about Johnny and Edwina; not unless I had to. I said instead:

"Want a cup of tea, Mike?" then walked slowly and stiffly into the kitchen without waiting for his answer.

He followed me and settled himself at the table companionably. Then he grinned teasingly.

"That's a beauty of a bruise you've got on your cheek," he said with mock seriousness.

"And for your information, Doctor," I retorted, "it feels like the whole of my body is coloured to match it."

"Pain still bad then?"

Mike's voice was sympathetic.

"Any sudden headaches or sickness, Kathy?"

I shook my head.

"No clamminess . . .?"

"No, Mike, just plain old-fashioned cuts and bruises and a sense of wonder that I'm alive to tell the tale."

Mike looked at me seriously for a moment and I held his eyes, unblinking, willing him to take it from there.

"And there *is* something to tell, isn't there, Kathy?"

"Yes," I nodded, relieved beyond measure to be able to unburden myself to him yet again. "There's a great deal to tell, Mike. It's all making sense, now."

"Like to talk about it?"

I took down mugs from the dresser, selecting the colours with exaggerated care, playing for time. That I would have to talk to someone was without dispute, but how much to tell was another matter. I took a deep breath then rushed in blindly.

"I know about the money now, Mike. The fourteen thousand pounds; I know where it came from."

Carefully I poured the tea, my eyes downcast. Mike didn't speak and I was grateful to him.

"Johnny and another man—a man called McIlroy—got it for doing a job. That was why Johnny disappeared—he wanted McIlroy off his back and all the money for himself," I went on flatly.

"How did you find out, Kathy?"

"McIlroy," I said simply.

"He came here? How did he know where to find you?"

"I don't know," I lied, disliking myself for not telling the whole truth and to Mike especially. "Anyway, he found me and guessed Johnny would arrive too, sooner or later, I suppose."

"Did he threaten you, this McIlroy?"

"Not really. His quarrel was with Johnny and I had the sense not to let him know that the money was in my name. He told me to give a message to Johnny—that was why I went out. That's how I fell. I missed my footing in the fog."

I stopped, for my voice was trembling and my hands had started to shake at the memory of it all.

"You mean you deliberately went out looking for your husband, knowing what you did?" Mike asked incredulously. "For heaven's sake—if you'd met him . . ."

"I did meet him, Mike. Well, not exactly *met* him," I interrupted. "The fog came down thick again and then I heard Johnny calling me. I was so afraid but I thought if I told him that McIlroy was looking for him, he'd maybe go away and leave Edwina and me in peace."

I took a gulp of tea. It was hot on my throat and made me choke. I was near to tears and Mike must have sensed it. He reached for my hand and held it tightly.

"Take your time," he said softly.

I gulped loudly then said:

"Look, Mike, to cut a long story short, Johnny kept calling. I followed the sound of his voice, then fell over the edge of the ravine. I think he meant me to do that. I think that if I hadn't fallen accidentally, he'd have—"

I started to sob quietly.

"I'm sorry, Mike. It's a wicked thing to think and Johnny's dead now, but I'm sure he meant me harm. And after I'd fallen, he didn't try to help me. He just laughed and whistled."

I felt the pressure of Mike's hand on mine. It seemed to tell me he didn't disbelieve my story.

I stared at the table-top for what seemed an age and all the time Mike sat there, waiting for me to go on.

"Last night," I whispered, "after you had left, Johnny came to the house. Edwina gave him money and the car keys—that's when it happened."

"He demanded money?"

"No, Mike. Not exactly."

I had to pick my words carefully.

"Johnny had been in touch with Edwina. He told her he was in trouble. I didn't know about it at the time, but what he said to her tied up with what McIlroy told me. Anyway, Johnny told Edwina he needed money. She gave him five hundred pounds, so he would leave Slaidbeck, I think."

"And he took the money and the car, then skidded into the wall?"

"It wasn't quite like that, Mike. After you came—when you sent Edwina and me back into the house—Dickie was standing by the door. He told me he'd tried to stop Johnny taking the car. He might have caused Johnny to swerve."

"I see," Mike said seriously.

"Is there any need to say anything about it? I don't want to involve Dickie. It's not certain, is it, that he caused the crash? I don't think I would have told you," I shrugged, "except that Edwina heard him tell me."

"We'll wait until the police have measured up and made their report. They couldn't do anything last night, Kathy, But they'll be back as soon as it's light. At the moment, it's an accident they're investigating."

He stopped and looked at me meaningfully. He'd given me a cue and I had to take it.

"Yes, Mike, but there's a lot more to it than that, isn't there? There's a lot of money in my bank and it's dishonest money. I don't want it—I'm not entitled to it, but whose money is it? Legally and morally, who should that money be returned to?"

"Have you no idea at all where it came from?"

"None, except that it's what was left from money given to Johnny and McIlroy for smuggling bullion and emeralds into the country. I don't know how they got the stuff past Customs, but the emeralds were stolen and they were worth a hundred thousand pounds."

Mike's head jerked up and he whistled through his teeth.

"So it *is* more than an accident the police have got on their hands, isn't it, Kathy?"

"Yes," I nodded miserably, "and are they going to believe me when I tell them I had nothing to do with it? I could be in a mess, Mike, a real mess. Either way, it's got to come out. Even if I wanted to keep quiet about the money—and I don't—I'd have McIlroy and goodness knows who else to contend with."

I laughed then, briefly and bitterly.

"You know, Mike, I thought seriously at one time that I'd just draw all the money out of the bank and give it to some charity. Stupid of me, wasn't it?"

"Well, not such a good idea, really, considering it wasn't yours to give away."

"Oh, I know that, but what do I do about it?"

"You tell the police at once. Can anyone corroborate what you've told me?"

"Yes. Edwina and the bank manager. The bank manager had his suspicions, I'm sure of it, and I told Johnny in front of Edwina that I knew about McIlroy and the emeralds and he didn't deny it."

Mike walked into the sitting-room and picked up the phone, but I stopped him.

"Look, Mike—before you do anything, there's something I didn't tell you. McIlroy's staying at the Swan. He said Johnny was to get in touch with him there."

"Which means he'll be gone now."

"But why? He might still be there, and if the police can pick him up—"

"Kathy, this is Slaidbeck," Mike retorted with over-emphasised patience. "Nothing much happens here so a car crash and the arrival of an ambulance and fire-engine wouldn't go unnoticed. The news would be in the public bar at the Swan within minutes. McIlroy could be miles away now, especially if he had a car with him."

"He did have a car," I confirmed. "Don't you think they'd know the number of it at the Swan? And I think he worked for the same firm as Johnny's. I know for certain he was an oil-man. He shouldn't be too hard to get hold of."

Mike picked up the phone again.

"Look, I know the local C.I.D. Inspector. I think it's a

169

matter for him. I think he should be told at once," Mike said, dialling a number.

As he waited for an answer he looked at me very gently and said:

"I'm sorry, Kathy, but we've got to tell the police about it. You do understand, don't you?"

I nodded and drew in a deep breath.

"Yes, Mike. I understand."

I walked back into the kitchen then and turned on the taps. I didn't want to hear what Mike said and I wanted that Mike should be able to say what had to be said without feeling any embarrassment for me. Johnny was dead but he had committed a serious crime. In simple language, Johnny was a criminal and that made me the wife—the widow—of a criminal. Not only that, I had fourteen thousand pounds to explain away. I hoped with all my heart the police would believe me.

I wanted to laugh out loud with sheer disgust and frustration. Stupid little fool that I was, I'd even let myself get fond of Mike Carter. I'd bet anything, I thought bitterly, that after today Mike just wouldn't be able to get away fast enough. I visualised a crowded court-room and Mike giving evidence for the Crown.

"*. . . the defendant consulted me professionally. She was in a highly emotional state at the time and confided in me that she knew her husband wasn't missing and that she thought he meant to harm her. She also told me she thought she was losing her reason . . .*"

And when it was all over—even if I got away without so much as a stain on my character—Mike wouldn't want to know. People like me were an embarrassment.

There was a movement behind me and I turned to see Edwina standing there. Her eyes were half-closed and her eyelids swollen from weeping. She fumbled in one of the dresser drawers and brought out a pair of dark glasses.

Briefly she wiped them on her dressing-gown, then placed them over her tell-tale eyes.

"There now," she said tightly, "that's better. I never could cry prettily — remember, Kathy? I suppose that's why I hardly ever indulge in tears."

"Sit down," I said gently. "I'll make you a coffee."

She nodded her thanks.

"What's Mike doing?" she asked. "Who's he talking to?"

"He's on to the C.I.D. He knows about McIlroy, Edwina, and the emeralds and the money in my bank. It's no use — it might as well come out sooner than later."

Edwina looked at me resignedly without speaking, then shrugged her shoulders as if she didn't care and wouldn't care about anything again.

"It's all right, I told her. "You've no need to worry. I didn't tell Mike about — well, about you and Johnny. No one need ever know, as far as I'm concerned, but what McIlroy'll say, though, if they pick him up, I don't know."

Edwina shrugged again. It was obvious to me that one way or another she didn't care who knew. She had loved Johnny deeply and now he was dead. That was all she was capable of feeling. I wanted to comfort her, but I didn't know how.

"Edwina?" I said gently, and when she raised her head to look at me I smiled. It was all I could do, but I think she understood and a little answering smile quirked briefly on her lips.

"I *did* love him," she said flatly.

I heard Mike's footsteps and we could say no more. I think I was glad, really. There wasn't anything more to say.

"Hi there, Edwina," Mike smiled. "How are you feeling?"

"Damned awful," she retorted. "Want a coffee?"

"Yes, please. My tea's gone cold, but it'll have to be a quick one. I've got a surgery to see to."

171

Then, turning to me, he said:

"A man from C.I.D. will be up straight away and they'll send a man to the Swan, just in case."

I nodded and said:

"Okay, Mike. Thanks a lot."

"It'll be all right. Don't worry, Kathy. Just tell the police all you told me—and anything else you and Edwina can remember. I'm certain they'll realise that neither of you are implicated."

He took a gulp of the coffee, then smiled apologetically.

"Ouch! That's hot! Afraid I'll have to leave it. I'm running late . . ."

I followed him to the front door.

"You'll be back, Mike? I know it's a lot to ask, but I'd be grateful—we'd both be grateful."

"Of course—just as soon as I can. Oh, and I've got to tell you this. It's likely they'll want to know the name of Johnny's dentist."

"His dentist? Why, Mike?"

Mike placed his hands gently on my shoulders.

"Yes, Kathy. You see, it's the only way they'll be able to identify him with absolute certainty—from a record of his teeth . . ."

I felt a shudder of distaste and spittle rose in my mouth. I hadn't realised it had been that awful.

"Sorry, but you had to know," Mike said, "and if any further identification is necessary, let me know and I'll be with you."

Tears filled my eyes at his goodness. I whispered:

"Oh, Mike, what would I have done without you?"

Gently he placed his forefinger beneath my chin, mindful in his concern for my bruised face.

"Come on now," he smiled. "Chin up, Kathy. I'll be back."

He was gone then and I stood quite still, listening to the

click of the garden gate, the opening and shutting of his car door, with a feeling of utter desolation. We were alone again, Edwina and I, and soon the police and the C.I.D. would be arriving. We'd have to lay our souls bare then, ours and Johnny's.

Slowly I walked back to the kitchen, to Edwina. I didn't know how either of us would get through the next few days. All that was certain was that we must face it together, she and I.

TWELVE

If I had thought Mike Carter would be a fair-weather friend, I was completely wrong. He was with Edwina and I when we made our statements to the police and the C.I.D. officers, and it was Mike who passed on the news that McIlroy's car had been found abandoned beside the M6 motorway; that McIlroy himself had been picked up by the Birmingham police.

It had come to light, the Inspector said later, that McIlroy had a police record; that he had served a prison sentence for assault and that I had been very lucky he had not used violence towards me. I wondered with a shiver, how different it might have been had I not had the sense to keep the whereabouts of the money quiet. Both Edwina and I were cleared of any complicity in the matter but were told we would be required to appear later to give evidence for the Crown at McIlroy's prosecution.

"I think," I said, after everyone had left and Edwina and I sat alone again in the lamplight, "that the Inspector rather enjoyed his bit of one-upmanship—giving the Metropolitan Police a lead on the emeralds, I mean."

Edwina shrugged her shoulders.

"Hmm. I wonder where they are now—on the Continent, I shouldn't wonder. Got Interpol running round like scalded cats, most likely. I wish Johnny had never seen them," she said vehemently. "I hope they never find the wretched things."

"An emerald choker and diamond and emerald ear-drops," I mused, quoting the official description. "They've probably been broken up by now."

"And the oil sheik who owned them will have hardly noticed their loss," Edwina added, bitterness evident in her voice.

"I'll be glad when the courts decide about the money," I said, trying to make small-talk, to change the subject. "I don't care where it goes—just so long as they take it away from me."

But Edwina was gazing into the fire. She had withdrawn into herself again. She was probably thinking, I supposed, that whenever she saw the bright green brilliance of an emerald, the wound of Johnny's death would bleed afresh inside her. Or was she thinking of the inquest to come and the ordeal that would follow in the wake of the Coroner's findings?

"Why did he do it, Kathy!" she demanded suddenly, lifting her chin from her hands. "I mean, why should he start smuggling in the first place? He had a decently paid job. He wasn't in any money trouble, was he?"

"I think he did it for the sheer devilry of it," I answered, biting my tongue on my lies, trying to keep what I was almost sure was the real truth from her.

Johnny had loved Edwina in his own way, but Edwina had made an undoubted success of life and earned a great deal more money than Johnny had ever done. The emerald-smuggling must have been the start of a get-rich-quick effort, an offer that someone of Johnny's temperament could never have turned down. McIlroy, I supposed, had been the instigator, the go-between. McIlroy had a record, didn't he? He'd probably done it before.

Edwina jumped to her feet then stood uncertainly, clenching and unclenching her fingers.

"Mike will be there tomorrow, won't he, Kathy—at the inquest, I mean. I don't think I can go through with it if he's not there."

"He'll be there," I replied, as evenly as I could. "He saw

a lot of it — he'll have to make a statement."

"I hope so. Oh, I hope so!"

She was like a cornered wild animal, tense and aggressive. Her grief seemed to have been replaced by bitterness; I wondered how much longer it would be before she broke down completely. It was strange that her distress gave me the courage to keep my own feelings in check.

I took her hand and held it in mine. I had done that a lot, I realised, over the past two awful days. Was I doing it to comfort her or did the clasping of our hands join our separate sorrows and help make them a little more bearable? Each of us had loved Johnny and that loving and the suffering it brought us would bond Edwina and I for all time. Already I had found it within me to forgive her.

"You're worn out," I said gently. "Let me make us both a hot drink? Perhaps tonight we'll be able to sleep a little better."

Edwina nodded, but we both knew that the night before us would be long and wakeful and immeasurably sad.

Throughout the unreal and unhappy days that followed, Mike's kindness gave a strange strength to Edwina and me. It was Mike who helped us through the inquest, and he, too, who guided us through the sad ceremonial that is the giving back of the dead. Mike's support was always there when we needed it, and as we followed Johnny to the little churchyard beside the old stone church, Mike was with Edwina and I at the graveside.

There were few to watch Johnny's going, I thought sadly. Just the three of us and the tired-looking old priest.

The sky mourned with us that morning, for even the clouds were heavy and grey. I wished as I walked away that the piping of a bird, perhaps, or a brief, pale shaft of winter sunlight could have promised a small gentle uplifting of hope for the future, but there was nothing to ease my unhappy heart.

A little part of me went with Johnny that day, for it is not possible, I found, for love to wholly die. I must try, I determined, to remember the good days, the times we had loved. I must never forget that Johnny's mind had been sick and that the man who now lay beneath the wide, wild hills was deserving of my pity.

Always Edwina was by my side like a small, pale wraith, lost in a wilderness of misery. I grieved that she should suffer so. I couldn't find it in my heart to be bitter that she and Johnny had deceived me. Perhaps, I thought, it had been I who deceived myself.

"Will you stay with me for a little while longer?" Edwina asked that night.

"Do you think it would be wise?" I replied, gently as I could.

She shrugged her shoulders in a helpless gesture and gave a desolate little laugh.

"Who is wise enough to know what is wise?" she asked, obliquely. "I'd like to think that at least you had forgiven me, Kathy."

"Oh, yes, Edwina, I have; please believe me. And I'm sure things will come right between us in time."

"You don't blame me too much, then, for breaking up your marriage?"

I could find nothing in my heart for her but pity.

"No, Edwina. I think perhaps that Johnny and I never truly loved. We'll get over it in time, you and I. We'll come to terms with it."

"You think so, Kathy? You really believe that?"

"I really believe it," I said.

I wished I could have been as sure as I sounded, for Edwina would never forget, I knew it. She would always keep a small, secret corner of her heart for Johnny.

Edwina's love had been constant. It had not wavered or doubted as mine had done. Edwina had not been in love with love.

"I must get back to London soon," I said. "There are things to be done. And I've got to learn to stand on my own two feet, now."

"When will you go?"

"Tomorrow, I think. It's best that I should. You'll be all right, won't you?"

"Yes, Kathy. I'll be all right."

There was a stubborn set to her mouth again and I saw an almost unconscious lifting of her shoulders. Edwina might grieve but no one would ever know about it.

"I'll come back," I said. "Perhaps, when spring is here and all this unhappiness is behind us, I'll come back, if you'd like it."

I realised that night as I moved quietly about my room packing my cases, that come tomorrow I would be leaving Slaidbeck and all its memories behind me. I wondered if, with the passing of time, Edwina and Mike might become closer. Would it be such a good thing, I asked myself, for me to return to this little village of memories both happy and sad? Wouldn't it be wiser if the break was sharp and clean? Could I, feeling as I had done about Mike — as I still felt, if I would admit it — lay myself open again to heartbreak? Michael Carter did not, I was almost sure, hold any feelings for me other than those of friendship. Nothing he had done could in any way lead me to hope that perhaps one day we would find happiness together. That I could love Mike with all my heart for the rest of my life meant nothing when Mike did not love me. It was as simple as that.

From now on I was alone. The thought was a dreary one. I wished our son could have lived and realised with a sense of blessed relief that the old familiar stabbing of pain I had always felt at recalling his loss was no longer there. Perhaps, I thought, I had wept all the bitterness from my heart the night that Johnny died.

I snapped out the light and walked over to the window. In the distance I could see the constant hills and nearer, solid and timeless, the tower of the church, standing guard in the night.

"Goodnight, Johnny," I whispered, "and goodbye. God keep you . . ."

Edwina drew up carefully at the crossroads outside Slaidbeck village, then turned slowly to the right, manoeuvring the car with concentration.

"Are you all right, Edwina?"

She was driving a hire-car from the local garage and it was completely different to the one she had driven before, the one in which, just a week ago . . .

I closed down my thoughts. I had resolved to try to keep Johnny at the back of my mind until I could think clearly and dispassionately about him.

"Sure," Edwina replied with a shrug of her shoulders, then, shifting her body into a more comfortable position, she replied:

"Just give me a few miles to get the better of these gears and I'll be fine. She's a sluggish old thing, this one, after — "

She stopped abruptly and I realised why. This was the first time she had driven herself since the accident and I knew that when she bought another car it would be the same make, the same colour even, as her previous one. It would have to be. Edwina would forget Johnny only when she was too old to remember or to dream.

I looked about me, wondering if I would ever again return to Slaidbeck and Keeper's Cottage. I had promised

Edwina I would. Deep down inside me I wanted to, for now Edwina was all I had in the world, my sort-of sister.

It was ironic that on this day the whole world should be breathtakingly beautiful again. Pale sunlight criss-crossed the hills, creating a patchwork of green and brown and purple. The sky was a clear winter-blue and the few clouds that lazed across it were light and frosty-white. Even the air seemed to sparkle and I could see for miles around me. It seemed that the world was spreading its arms and saying:

"Here I am, Kathleen Parr. I'm big and wide and there's a whole new beginning for you if you have the courage to take it. I can be sad and dangerous and lonely, but I am generous and exciting, too, and there is warmth in me, and love and peace if you will let yourself find it."

I glanced again at Edwina. Her face had been pale, but the soft, coral-bright coat she now wore had given it a glow of warmth. It was a colour I liked but it didn't suit me; Johnny had said so.

"Don't wear that red again, Kathleen," he once demanded. "It fights with your hair."

I hadn't known at that time, but it must have been Edwina's colour and special to her.

I sighed irritably. It was over and done with, I told myself yet again. It had been over between Johnny and me could I but admit it, long before the day Edwina and Johnny first met. It was fact and nothing I could do would change it. I had to accept it and learn to live with it, without bitterness. Edwina and Johnny met too late, in exactly the same way I had met Mike Carter. People made mistakes the world over and it was no use sighing over them. It was sad; sadder still in my case, because Michael Carter didn't love me.

I tilted my chin and straightened my shoulders and looked again at the wild beauty of the world around me. I had been given another chance and I must grasp it eagerly. I was young and I would learn to forget, I vowed fiercely. The bad memories would fade and the good ones — the memories of Mike — would become bearable once I had learned to accept life and face it alone.

We passed the signpost that said, *Skipton — 10 miles.* Edwina had mastered the strange car now and was pushing it to the utmost of its aged limits. I glanced into the rear mirror and saw nothing but the misty distance. Slaidbeck was slipping farther and farther behind us. Soon it would be just a dot on a map in a faraway northern county.

We had driven through it at first light, seeing no one but the milkman and the red postal-delivery van. I had half-turned to look down the High Street to catch a glimpse of Mike's surgery, but his car was not standing outside and the windows were not lit. Mike was out on a call, I thought, disappointed.

I had telephoned his surgery before leaving Keeper's Cottage. I wanted to say goodbye to him, to thank him for all he had done, hear his slow, comfortable voice just once more before I left. But there had been only an answering anonymous voice, asking me to record my message, and I had whispered that I was leaving, replacing the receiver reluctantly and sadly. When I reached London, I reasoned, I could write him a letter of thanks. It would be the most sensible thing to do. It was, I knew, the only thing to do. I had merely to ask myself the question that had so often been pushed into my subconscious to get things into their proper perspective:

Why had Mike Carter never married?

He was attractive — oh, there was no denying that. He was gentle and protective and manly. He danced well; he made a woman feel good, just to be with him. He had a comfortable country practice in a quaint little Yorkshire village. He had everything, I told myself miserably, so why was he single? Why hadn't he been snapped up long ago? Was it because the woman he wanted had only given him friendship? Had that woman been in love with another man—a married man—and had Mike been content with that friendship; content to wait and to hope that one day that woman would turn to him? Was Mike in love with Edwina?

I tried to think of the little things, like the easy way they spoke together, the accepted arrangement that Mike ate regularly at Edwina's place, the fact that he had been with us constantly during the past awful week. I had imagined his kindness had been for me, but it would have been principally for Edwina's benefit. Mike's solicitude was surely meant for her, truth known, not for me. Would they come together now? In time, would Edwina let herself love again and would it be Mike she loved?

What would happen then to my glib promise to come back to Slaidbeck? How could I bear to see them together, stand lonely outside their new-found happiness? I'd been blind as a bat not to see it before. How could Mike Carter—any man, indeed—look twice at me when there was Edwina for the loving?

Suddenly I wanted to be gone and was glad when I recognised the outskirts of Skipton. In a little while we would drive down the long, cobble-sided main street, circle the roundabout, and in a matter of minutes would be at the station. I was impatient to get away from my stupid hopes and fantasies. I would never, I resolved, return to Slaidbeck. I was too weak. It would be physically impossible.

Edwina stopped the car outside the station entrance and unloaded my cases.

"Wait there," she said briefly, then drove the car to the parking lot. I fumbled in my purse for the return half of

my ticket as I waited for her to come back. I could see my
train standing already at the platform. I wanted to be on
my way, leave everything behind me. I'd been so foolish it
was almost laughable. Mike Carter and *me*?

"Change at Leeds," said the man at the barrier,
snipping my ticket.

I turned to Edwina.

"Edwina—please don't come on to the platform with
me. I don't like being seen off. I've got a thing about it."

I blushed awkwardly. I wasn't being truthful. Usually I
liked being met or waved on my way, but this time it was
different. I didn't want to stand with Edwina, see her
brooding sorrow, not know what to say that might help.
And if she asked me again when I would be coming back
to Slaidbeck, if she tried to hold me to my promise to
return in the spring, how could I lie to her?

"Are you sure, Kathy! I could come with you as far as
Leeds . . .?"

She placed the glossy magazines and chocolates she had
just bought into my arms.

". . . It wouldn't be any trouble, honestly."

"Thanks," I returned, "but I'll be all right on my own,
truly I will."

I wanted to be on the train, to be alone with my
dejection. I had hoped to wish Mike goodbye and had been
disappointed to find him out. Inside me I had been stupid
enough to hope that he might yet appear from out of
nowhere, if only to say goodbye and wish me luck.

I picked up my cases and pushed through the barrier.
Mike wouldn't come. There was no reason at all why he
should.

"Don't wait," I said again to Edwina.

I leaned over and kissed her cheek. I had the feeling that
she, too, wanted to play it my way. She stood for a moment
looking at me with a strange sadness in her eyes.

"I'll see you?" she whispered.

"One day," I answered gravely. "One day, perhaps."

Then I smiled at her and she lifted her hand in a small, lonely gesture, turning abruptly away. I watched the brave walk and the tilt of her head as she crossed over to where she had parked the car, but she did not turn round.

The little local train slipped smoothly away from the platform. I closed my eyes tightly as it did so. I didn't want to see the little stone houses or the distant hills, glimpse a faraway stretch of moorland. I didn't want to look at anything that would remind me of Slaidbeck, where Mike would now have started morning surgery, just as he always did.

"I'll see you?" Edwina had asked, but I knew I would never have the courage to return to Keeper's Cottage. I couldn't see Mike again, be reminded of my foolish hopes. I half-hoped that the police wouldn't be able to make a case against McIlroy. I wouldn't be forced to meet Mike again then. If they didn't find the emeralds, surely there could be no prosecution?

I didn't open my eyes until I knew the little market town was far behind me.

There was no one sitting near me and I was glad. It meant I didn't have to talk to anybody or smile at anybody. I looked at my hands, then at my handbag, my feet, the back of the seat in front of me; anywhere but out of the window of the compartment. I didn't want to see the crisp winter landscape, take away with me any memory that would help remind me of Johnny or Edwina or Mike. I had to count my blessings. What a glib, easy phrase that was, I thought impatiently; how hard to put into practice.

But I would try to count them, for all that. Things like the verdict of accidental death that had been returned without involving Dickie Hatburn in any way. The car had skidded beyond any doubt on a patch of wet mud, churned up by some tractor or deposited there by the wheels of a farm cart. I had been lucky too in that the police had unreservedly believed that I had had no part in or knowledge of the theft of the emeralds or in bringing them into the country. The worst that could happen now was that I might have to make an appearance in court if McIlroy was prosecuted. They hadn't got a lead on the emeralds yet but they would, the C.I.D. Inspector had said with satisfaction; they would! And if they did, Johnny would be on trial, too, I thought miserably. He would be referred to as *the deceased* and he would bear the brunt of McIlroy's lies and evasions.

I shuddered with distaste at the mere idea of it all, but I was glad that no one had learned about Edwina and Johnny. Nor would they, I thought grimly, if it rested with me. Edwina deserved another chance to be happy. It was almost certain, I thought, that one day she would find it — with Mike Carter.

Mike. I wondered what he would be doing now. My mind winged back happily to his homely surgery and the little back room where we drank mugs of instant coffee and ate Mrs Hatburn's fruit cake. Just about two weeks ago, my mind supplied; a lifetime away.

It had been silly of me to hope Mike might have wished me goodbye or even seen me off at the station. But then, I'd always been foolish and timid and , compared with Edwina, insignificant and colourless. Edwina. Lonely, brittle and tragic, who would find love again.

I had nearly an hour to wait at Leeds station. The morning rush seemed almost to be over yet it was still noisy and crowded and for me, unbearably lonely.

I checked in my cases then bought a cup of tea. I found myself an empty table then glanced through the magazines

Edwina had given me. The pages flicked over like a coloured fan and I saw nothing that was printed on them.

It would be good, I mused, if I could wish Mike through the cafeteria door. He could be wearing his tweed jacket and his pipe would be sticking out of his top pocket. He'd be wearing his shabby old scarf, too, wound carelessly around his neck. Then he would catch my eye and smile and bring his drink to the table at which I was sitting. And after we had talked, after I had thanked him for all he had done, he would carry my cases to the train and find me a corner seat by the window. Throughout it all, of course, I'd be very calm and ordinary and my heart wouldn't beat madly and my eyes wouldn't shine like those of a schoolgirl in love.

I looked towards the door but Mike wasn't standing beside it and it remained steadfastly closed. Doors never opened for day-dreaming fools.

I looked at my watch. I had only managed to waste ten minutes. I sighed petulantly and, pushing aside the tea I hadn't wanted anyway, I walked to the bookstall and the rows of paperback editions of romantic novels on show there. Earnestly I read each title, shrugging inwardly. Real love stories, the ones that always ended hopefully and happily, were for other women, not for me.

A voice announced that the Yorkshire Pullman would leave in twenty minutes' time at ten-thirty hours. Almost thankfully, yet strangely reluctant, I made my way to the left-luggage to pick up my cases. I wondered what had gone wrong with my wish. Mike should have come to the cafeteria wearing his old coat and scarf. He should have smiled as if he'd known he would meet me there. It was all wrong. My mouth was dry. I hadn't thought it would go dry. It wasn't Mike standing there, was it? Not Mike Carter, wearing a grey lounge suit and carrying a briefcase. Mike didn't look like a city lawyer, so it couldn't be him.

But for all that, my heart started to beat madly like it shouldn't have done and I knew there was laughter and disbelief and happiness in my eyes as I called:

"Mike! Oh, Mike—what on earth . . .?"

The grey-suited unfamiliar figure turned and smiled then hurried towards me, and I knew then. It *was* Mike and he *was* here. Why, I didn't know; and how, I didn't care. I only knew it would be all right, now; that I could wish him goodbye and thank him as I had wanted to do and maybe for just a few precious minutes, talk to him.

"Kathy! I thought I'd missed you!"

My heart almost burst with tenderness as he smiled again, brushing away the shock of hair that fell across his forehead in that dear, familiar gesture.

"What are you doing here?" I almost laughed. "You should be taking morning surgery!"

I wasn't being calm and ordinary and friendly and I didn't care.

"I've been playing truant," he grinned. "I spent the night in Leeds at a reunion dinner. Got a *locum* from the hospital to stand in for me."

"But how did you know I'd be here?"

"I phoned Slaidbeck this morning to see if there was anything urgent at the surgery. The *locum* told me there was nothing that couldn't wait until I got back except a message from someone called Kathy. So I decided to take a chance on your getting the 10.30 to London. I met the Skipton train in—I must have missed you."

"It doesn't matter, Mike. You've found me now and I'm so glad you did," I breathed, all pretence gone

Mike took the luggage-ticket I was holding in my hand.

"Let's get your cases and settle you on the train," he said easily. "There's still a few minutes left. I want to talk to you."

I followed him happily, smiling at the ticket-collector as if he were a long-lost friend.

"This one'll do, Mike."

I ducked into the first compartment with an open door. We had about fifteen minutes left. They were very precious and I didn't want to waste them in selecting a seat.

Mike placed my luggage on the rack then came to stand with me on the platform. It was, I thought, the most beautiful station platform in the world. And everyone seemed to be smiling and there wasn't a cold wind blowing because it wasn't November. Mike had come to say goodbye and I'll swear that birds sang all around us and lilac bloomed.

"Kathy," Mike said softly. He was looking into my eyes very tenderly. "This is difficult for me to say because it really isn't the right time for me to be saying it."

He gave a little smile.

"I'm not managing very well," he said, rubbing the back of his neck as he always did when he was stuck for words.

"You see, I know it wouldn't be fair of me to intrude — not yet. There's sad things you've got to forget and I hope there are some happy ones that you'll want to remember, but . . ."

"Yes, Mike?" I whispered.

"Well, I'll be in London, I hope, in early January, and maybe by then you'll have got over everything . . ."

Suddenly my heart was beating joyfully and every pulse in my body throbbed with happy anticipation. We were wasting precious time. Oh, how we were wasting it!

"There's a series of medical lectures I'd like to go to, Kathy. I've not taken a real break in ages and the locum who stands in for me is always pretty anxious for jobs so it's almost certain I'll be able to make it."

I held my breath. I couldn't speak for joy. It was surging inside me with such force that I didn't know what to do.

"Well, I wondered if I could phone you when I'm down? My evenings will be free so perhaps we could have a meal or see a show or two. Would you like that, Kathy?"

"Yes, Mike, I would. I'd like it very much."

He gave a brief grin of relief. He looked at that moment like a small, eager boy.

"Well, then . . ." he hesitated.

Suddenly I was very sure of myself and very sure for both of us.

"I'll give you my address, Mike. You'll want that."

I fumbled in my handbag. Oh, how the minutes were flying past!

"Here's an envelope addressed to me. You'll get my number, if you want it, from the phone book."

I gave it to him and our hands touched briefly, warmly. I said:

"Mike—take care of Edwina. She needs a friend right now."

"Yes, Kathy." He smiled gently into my eyes. "I think I understand, now. She's a one-man girl, but she'll be all right, in time."

I sensed that Mike knew or at least suspected the truth, but it didn't matter because now I knew that some day I would tell him—all of it. It would only be right that he should know. There would be no secrets between us.

There was a banging of doors and the urgent sound of a whistle.

I stepped on to the train. Mike slammed the door shut, and I leaned out.

"Thanks, Mike," I whispered, my voice thick with happiness. "Thanks for everything."

Mike laid his hand on mine and my heart did another joyful somersault. He didn't kiss me. Like he said, it wasn't the right time. Later, we would both know just when.

"You'll write, Kathy?"

"I'll write," I said. "I'll write as soon as I get back to London."

"Yes; I'll want to know you've arrived safely."

The train was moving now.

"Take care until I see you, Kathy. Look after yourself, darling."

I watched from the window until he was almost out of sight. Then he raised his hand and I knew he was still smiling.

I sank into my seat, my legs weak with happiness, my heart singing like a bird when a storm is over.

There were tears in my eyes now;tears of joy and love and hope. I blinked them away and looked out of the window. All around me the chimneys stood tall and dark; the roof-tops grimy and cheerless. I closed my eyes and in my mind I was back in Slaidbeck again. I saw the hills and suddenly they were my hills, their dark aloofness gone. Now they were wishing me well, calling me back to them. There was a happiness around me so complete that I felt I would cry out with joy.

"Goodbye, hills," I whispered. "I *will* see you again. I'll come back soon, to where my heart is."

It seemed right then, in that breathless moment of wonder, through the grey gloom of the city, that the sun should suddenly shine.